NO GODS
ONLY CHAOS

Sobelo
Books

SOBELO BOOKS

2024

ISBN (Paperback): 978-1-965389-00-3
ISBN (eBook): 978-1-965389-01-0
Sobelo Books
P.O. Box 726
7890 Richmond Rd,
Toano VA, 23168
www.sobelobooks.com

Cover Artwork © 2024 by Truborn Design
Interior Design © 2024 by Brady Moller
Cover Wrap Design © 2024 Desert Isle Design, LLC

NO GODS
ONLY
CHAOS

L. P. HERNANDEZ

Cemetery Joe (Picnic in the Graveyard, *Cemetery Gates Media*)

Hesitation Cuts (Institutionalized, *Sinister Smile Press*)

The Bystander (Human Monsters, *Dark Matter Ink*)

From the Red Dirt (If I Die Before I Wake V, *Sinister Smile Press*)

Under No Circumstances (Unpublished)

Urbex (Unpublished)

Offerings to an Old God (Monster Lairs, *Dark Matter Magazine*)

The Final Gift (Unpublished)

The Last of Our Kind (Unpublished)

Only Ever Night (Lockdown Horror #1, *Black Hare Press)*

The Return of the Champion (Unpublished)

Family Annihilator (If I Die Before I Wake VII, *Sinister Smile Press*)

The Last Chance Diner (Black Rainbow, *NBH Publishing*)

For Mom, who helped me believe I was good at this before it was true.

"CHAOS IS THE SCORE UPON WHICH REALITY IS WRITTEN."

—Henry Miller, *Tropic of Cancer*

CONTENTS

CEMETERY JOE

Spend enough time around dead bodies and you're bound to end up with a nickname you would not have chosen yourself. Joe Lindale was known as *Cemetery Joe* in town, with *more like Corpse-Fucker Joe* offered as a witty retort usually met with wisps of laughter. He lived in defiance of God, skin as gray as the bologna forgotten in a backpack for the summer, fingers like anatomical models of the skeleton. He stank of death, of dirt and the pollen of memorial flower arrangements. He had a candy cane for a spine, broken concrete for teeth, and hair so thin it might as well have been an aura.

Everyone had an opinion. For Juan, George, and Eric, Cemetery Joe was a constant source of speculation.

On an otherwise boring July night sandwiched between sophomore and junior years, and with nothing better to do, idle speculation evolved into a plan.

"There's no way he fucks dead bodies," George said.

"How would you know?" Eric asked, voice monotone as he watched his avatar get tea-bagged by a child screaming German obscenities through his headset.

"He would have been caught. Right?" George asked, looking to Juan for affirmation.

Juan wiped energy drink dew from his ghost of a mustache and relived a grocery store encounter with Joe weeks previous.

"I'm not convinced he fucks corpses, but if he does he might just be really good at it."

"Good at fucking corpses?" George asked.

"No, good at not getting caught. I was in line behind him a while back. I don't remember what he was buying, normal old people stuff, but it was the way he looked at the cashier. Stacy I think? She was a senior last year?"

"Yeah, I know her," George said, recalling the day she wore white leggings with a black thong.

"The dude didn't blink, stared at her tits the whole time."

"Can't blame him for that," Eric said.

"Yeah, but then he starts biting his lip. Hard. Like the pain was keeping him from doing something else. His skin cracks and bleeds. By the time he checked out there was blood running down his neck. I don't think he even noticed. Creepy, but like I said, never been caught."

Eric tossed his headset onto the bed and swiveled in his gaming chair, "We could find out."

"What do you mean?" George asked.

"We could find out. We could go to the cemetery. He lives there, right? That little cabin-shack thing in the back?"

"Go there and do what?" Juan asked.

"Yeah, how would we find out? You gonna walk in on him two inches deep in Juan's dead grandma?" George chided.

Juan coughed energy drink into his fist, "Are you insulting *Joe* or my grandma?"

George frowned, "Hadn't thought it through."

The boys lobbed glances back and forth, faint German insults chirping through the headset.

"I dare you," Eric said, turning his attention to George.

"Dare me?"

"Dare him to do what?" Juan interjected.

George cleared his throat, sat up straighter on the bed, "Unless I walk in on him with Juan's grandma, I'm not gonna get any proof."

Eric shook his head, "Don't need to do that. Just take something of his."

George huffed, "Take something?"

Eric nodded, "Sneak into his shack and take something of his."

George rubbed his hands on his jeans, his smile twitching, "You dare me? What are we, ten?"

"You dared me to drink the bee that died in my Gatorade last week!" Eric said.

"Yeah, but…"

All eyes followed the sound of tinkling keys. Juan grinned, "I'll drive."

GEORGE TUGGED THE COLLAR OF HIS SHIRT, WATCHED THE suburbs melt into downtown. Streetlights dimmed with every block or disappeared altogether. The city had grown away from the cemetery over the years, leaving half-empty strip malls in the wake. Townhomes were carved up into apartments, backyards paved to accommodate the demand for parking. Churches upgraded to larger buildings closer to the suburbs and the congregations who fled there, their leftover campuses transitioning to community centers. AA meetings were held inside every Wednesday and meth was sold outside twenty-four hours a day.

"I mean, the door's probably gonna be locked, right?" George asked from the backseat.

"Guess we'll find out," Eric said.

"If it is just knock. Ask old Corpse-Fucker Joe if you can have a lighter or something."

George frowned at another unsuccessful effort to weasel out of the dare. It was **not** the same as drinking a bee. Not even close. He'd have to walk through a cemetery, alone, sneak into the shack of the man who, in his capacity as a mortician's assistant, would have seen Aunt Rita's dead body only two months previous. George was not close to his aunt but had attended the funeral. Corpse-Fucker Joe lingered on the periphery during the graveside service, shovel at the ready as if it was a personal goal to bury the casket before the family vacated the parking lot. If Joe *was* home George would need to convince him to part with something, which might have been a worse option.

George wondered if he could will himself to vomit. That would end it. He jabbed his belly a few times, but there wasn't much to work with. Some microwave popcorn and half a Dr. Pepper already snaking through his intestines.

"It won't prove he fucks dead people. Isn't that the point?" George said.

Juan glanced in the rearview, "Nah, now the point is you're shitting yourself and we're gonna have fun with it."

"Fuck you guys," George whispered, sinking low into the seat so the landmarks leading them to the cemetery were hidden.

"Do you really think he…" Eric began.

Juan shrugged, "Who knows? There was that guy everyone said got caught with a goat. Probably not true, but he *looked* like the kind of guy who would do something like that."

"Stu-u-u-uart," Eric bleated. "What an awful name."

Juan pulled into the funeral home parking lot and navigated to the far corner of it. The cemetery spread across thirty acres of land, of which about two-thirds was occupied or reserved for future burials. He reversed the car into a parking space and flipped the lights off.

"Can't see it from here, but from the street the cabin looked dark. You might luck out, George. Might be able to sneak in, grab a coaster and jet," Juan said.

"Light's on in the funeral home," Eric said. "Think Joe's at *work?*"

George grimaced at the implication, then took a steadying breath. Either he was going to do this or put a target on his back for the rest of the summer.

"Anything? Just…anything?" he asked.

"Yeah, I mean the cooler the thing is the more points you get," Juan said.

"Oh, we're tracking points now?" George said, unbuckling his seatbelt.

"Just started," Eric said, winking.

"Fuck you guys," George said.

He slammed the car door and shuffled across a parking lot still radiating heat from a day under the Texas sun. The blacktop gripped the soles of his shoes making it feel as if he was stepping in stiff mud. He was more frightened at the prospect of being accused of trespassing than of having a run-in with Joe. College wasn't far off and the last thing he needed was a criminal record.

"You've got family here, remember?" George whispered to himself. "If anyone asks, you're just here to pay respects."

It wasn't obvious the *anyone* George was concerned about. There were no other visitors at ten o'clock on a Tuesday night. The closest people to him, other than his friends in the car and possibly Joe in the funeral home, were three blocks away haggling over the price of meth. He glanced over his shoulder and saw both Juan and Eric's faces illuminated by the screens of their cell phones. Maybe he could just grab something on the way? Some of the headstones had mementos, coins and stuffed animals. George licked his lips. They felt like tree bark. He jammed his hands in his pockets and scanned the graves.

Why is my heart beating so fast? It's not illegal to be in a cemetery at night. No one is going to call the cops if...

He grazed the roughened crest of a headstone and threw a quick, casual glance behind. George cleared his throat and strayed off the walking path, eyes peeled for a trinket he could pocket. Something glinted silver and he bent to retrieve it.

"Ah shit," he said, dropping the foil wrapper on the grass.

The sounds of the town were muffled, distant, as if absorbed by the air around the cemetery. The chime of his cell phone, though, was harsh and abrupt, drawing a bark from him he was thankful his friends did not hear.

Juan: *We see you fucker. Eric says it has to be a spoon since ur trying to be clever.*

George turned. The car was some distance away, but the double middle fingers backlit by cell phone light were easy to spot. His head drooped, hands returning to pockets. He checked the funeral home lights and resumed his trek toward the shack.

In the car, Juan and Eric introduced a new dynamic to the night's activity.

"Hey, let's leave him," Eric said.

"What? No. He's already scared," Juan said.

"No, I mean, just make him *think* we're leaving him. Let's just drive down the road so he can't see the car. He'll shit himself! We'll drive back when he calls."

Juan pursed his lips. George was barely distinguishable from the lightly glowing tombstones to either side of him.

"Let's at least wait 'til he can't see us."

Eric nodded and resumed scrolling on his cell phone.

THE CABIN LOOKED LIKE FOUR SHEDS NAILED TOGETHER. The lights from the street did not touch it, and the moon was only a quarter full. Five feet from the front door, George might have believed it to be a two-dimensional silhouette. Behind, he could only see the roof of the funeral home, not the lights in its window. The parking lot was also hidden behind a slight rise in the terrain. George would have to rely on his friends to alert him if Joe left, and at that moment they were half a block down the street, giggling at the genius of their plan.

"Fuck it, just a spoon," George said, and turned the doorknob.

The hinges screamed like a succession of drowning cats and fingers of cool air groped his exposed skin. He stepped inside and quickly closed the door to the same horrific sound. George knew he would have to search in the dark, couldn't risk Corpse-Fucker seeing the light. He began to feel his way through the first room, eyes barely adjusting to the darkness. His shin collided with the edge of a coffee table, and it shrieked across the floorboards.

George's face pinched in pain, but he did not cry out. He felt his way into the adjoining room, hardly bigger than a walk-in closet, and found only a dining table with mismatched chairs. Where was his bedroom? Where was the kitchen? The Dr. Pepper and popcorn seemed to reverse course in their digestive journey, hot gushes of stomach acid sprinkling up his throat.

Back in the living room, George found a door with a staircase descending into black. He tested the first step, and it accepted his weight with only a mouse squeak of protest. Maybe the kitchen was in the basement? George took another step. How long had he been inside the shack, two minutes or five? Too long either way. Another step. George stopped, sniffed, a dusty-sweet scent tickling his nostrils.

He reached the bottom quicker than anticipated and stumbled, hands thrashing blindly in the dark. The basement doorway was a gray rectangle behind him. Surely Joe would not see if he used his cell phone for light? George baby-stepped into the room, the rosy odor reminiscent of the competing potpourri pots in his aunt's house. His thigh grazed what might have been a couch.

Sniffling, nose crinkling, George fished his cell phone out of his pocket. *If I can't find a spoon in this room I'm out of here.* The abuse from his friends was preferable to creeping through the flower-scented basement of a man nicknamed Corpse-Fucker. He pressed his index finger over the sensor.

"What the fuck?" he whispered, aiming his cell phone's screen at the far end of the basement.

"Mannequins?"

He stepped closer angling the phone's light to see better. It revealed the knees and shins of half a dozen mannequins, their torsos reclined and tilted away from the light. His heartbeat thrummed in his ear, chipmunk-sized breaths whistling past his lips. Despite the low light, George noticed there was hair on two sets of legs, a long pink scar on another, and a definitely-not-plastic hand resting on one knee.

"What the f…"

A sound to his left, like weight shifting on an old mattress. George turned his face and yipped as a cool, metallic cord brushed over his cheek. He seized it and pocketed his cell phone. The shape of the light fixture was just visible overhead. He could be quick about it, just a flash.

As he pulled the cord, cold fingers enveloped his hand.

CLICK

Every head turned toward him; every eye settled on his face. Fifteen people, maybe twenty seated on couches or on the floor. Some were undressed. One wore a pencil skirt with no top, another a white blouse with no bottoms. There was a middle-aged man in a tuxedo seated next to a middle-aged woman wearing a silk evening gown. A scream died halfway up his throat as he pivoted, certain Corpse-Fucker Joe was standing beside him.

He wasn't.

George's mouth, as dry a dead cat's litter box, hung open.

"Aunt Rita?" he gasped.

"THINK IT'S BEEN LONG ENOUGH?" JUAN ASKED.

"He hasn't called," Eric said.

"Yeah. That's what has me worried. This is taking too long. What if Joe walked in on him?"

Eric shrugged, "We can head back to see if the lights in the funeral home are on."

Juan pulled onto the street.

"What if he found something?"

"Like what?" Eric asked, looking up from his phone.

"I don't know. A picture?"

"Of him fucking a corpse?"

Eric shrugged, "Maybe?"

"Oh shit," Juan said, pulling into the funeral home parking lot. "The lights are off."

SHE WORE A MESH NEGLIGEE THAT HID NOTHING. AUNT RITA was only thirty-eight, and so an autopsy had been performed to determine the cause of death. The coroner's handiwork was visible between and above the breasts George struggled not to see. He jerked his hand free of his dead aunt's cold fingers. It felt as if his organs were playing musical chairs.

"...left the goddamned door open?"

George slowly pivoted toward the new voice, which rattled like an old truck engine.

Joe stood in the doorway at the head of the basement stairs.

George could not catch a breath. His heart beat furiously and the borders of his world grew fuzzy with blue light.

"Well, this is unexpected."

Joe grasped the bannister and walked down the stairs. The eyes, previously pasted to George, followed his descent.

Once he reached the basement floor, a woman with jet black hair in a Baywatch-style bathing suit sprang off the couch. She dropped to her knees in front of Joe and he gently nudged her away with his knee.

"Not right now, doll. That's Thursday, remember? Today is Tuesday."

The woman returned to the couch and Joe stepped forward. He squinted, his lips rolling like two slugs dowsed with salt.

"I remember you," he said, then glanced at Rita. "You were with her, right? I never forget a face. Oh, this must be a shock for you, huh?"

He stood a bit taller than George remembered, the hump in his back less severe. Though nothing about the man indicated strength or speed, George could not unglue his shoes to make a break for it.

"Corpse-Fucker. That's what they call me in town, huh?"

George licked his lips, eyes locked on the basement door. Joe nodded his head at something behind George. A moment later a hand the size of a Christmas ham clamped onto George's shoulder. He could *feel* the size of the man behind him, the gravity of a black hole.

"Good boy, Tony," Joe said with a wink to the black hole. "Can't let you go I'm afraid. You know for all the rumors you're the first person to actually find out?"

George attempted to lean forward, and the giant's fingers squeezed until George was certain the skin would rupture, and its fingertips would meet.

"Find out what?" George asked through gritted teeth.

Joe smiled and draped a skeleton hand on George's other shoulder.

"That it's true! Sort of."

Joe nodded at the giant and led George back to the center of the room. Aunt Rita found a place along the wall.

They were a menagerie of ages and shapes, though the oldest were roughly middle-aged. Women outnumbered men by about three to one. As George finally *saw* them the chaos in his guts reignited.

"Mrs. Andrews?" he whispered.

His third grade teacher did not blink when her name was spoken. She wore a beret (and nothing else), which would have covered the damage to her skull from the car accident two years previous. Otherwise, she looked exactly as he remembered her, save for the naked part.

"They *were* corpses. So, I guess that part was right. And I *do* fuck them, but they fuck each other, and me too. On Sundays only, though," Joe said, then turned his attention to a man on his left. "*Right*, Gary?"

The man nodded robotically.

Joe leaned into George and whispered, "He pretends to get his days mixed up."

George probed the space behind him with the toe of his shoe and it was roughly rebuffed by the giant named Tony.

"What are they? If they *were* corpses, what are they now?"

George knew it was important to keep him talking. Whatever his plans were, they would happen a lot sooner if George was silent.

Joe sucked in a large breath and folded his arms over his chest, "That's gonna take a minute. Why don't you have a seat?"

With a few snaps of his fingers an overstuffed chair was abandoned by its occupant, a redhead wearing denim overalls with the crotch missing. She walked in circles for a few seconds and then sat on the floor. George was shadowed by Tony as he sat in the chair.

"Get comfortable, yeah?" Joe said, then snapped his fingers again.

Aunt Rita left her place on the wall and moved behind George's chair. She began to massage his shoulders.

George shuddered and squeaked, "Can it be someone else?"

Thirty seconds later, George's dead third grade teacher went to work on the knots in his back.

"Where do you think you were before you were born?" Joe asked. He was sandwiched between the well-dressed couple on the couch.

"What do you mean?"

"Before you were alive. What *were* you, or were you nothing?"

George shook his head, not understanding.

"I don't know. Nothing I guess?"

Joe nodded, "I knew I was different growing up. This hump in my back isn't from old age or diggin' holes. It's from starin' at my shoes all day because I couldn't stand to look up."

"Why?"

"I saw what no one else did, no one else *does* to my knowledge."

"What's that?"

"Life."

"Life?"

"Well, the potential for it. It's all around us. It's in this room right now," Joe said, then leaned forward. "Life is potential. It's a pooled possibility."

"I don't-"

"A vapor. That's what it looks like to me. All different colors and densities. What it needs is a vessel. A fetus in utero. An apple seed just beginning to sprout. This vapor…it's just potential until it finds its vessel."

George nodded then shivered upon realizing he was angling his back so his dead teacher could better access the muscles.

"Some time ago, too late in life I'm afraid, I realized I could interact with it," Joe said, then held up a finger.

He aimed the finger above George's head, began to twirl it in lazy circles. The pressure on his back began to relent. Joe smiled and his finger gave a *come hither* motion. The hands on George's back went limp, and Mrs. Andrews slumped over the chair, hair falling over George's face like a curtain.

"It's very faintly pink. Like cotton candy. Like a sunset you would try to describe and fail miserably," Joe said finger still beckoning. "Quite beautiful."

He cleared his throat and resumed the spiral motion with his finger, reversing direction. With a flick of Joe's wrist, Mrs. Andrews stood as if rousing from a nap.

"I started with animals. Roadkill. I pulled this vapor out of the air and pushed it into the body. Remember that old story about the zombie raccoon by the YMCA?"

George nodded.

"That was me. I fucked that one up. Took three years to catch it. I learned about my gift, the right vapor for the right vessel to meet my needs."

George glanced at his nearly nude aunt, the fear mingling with anger.

Joe followed his gaze, "I get it. I get it. I would be upset, too. I won't try to justify it to you. I'm a sack of shit. Fine. But I'll tell you this, your aunt is dead. Think of it like a candle. The flame is snuffed out, but we still have all this beautiful wax. This vapor, it *wants* to live. Sure, this isn't living exactly, but it's better than floating through the Universe forever."

George nodded, crossed his arms.

"Why are you telling me this? You don't think I'll…"

"Go to the cops?" Joe said, then shook his head. "No. You won't. As for why I'm telling you. What else could I do but tell the truth? Obviously, I'm not smart enough to do some Frankenstein shit. But it's actually kinda therapeutic sharing my story."

"What makes you think I won't tell?"

Joe smiled big and rotten. He showed his gnarled finger, began to twirl it, then aimed it at George's chest.

"What an interesting color. Purple, kind of. Like your aunt."

George gasped and clutched at his heart. His legs went rigid.

"Wonder where I could send you. I could do a switcheroo, you know? Pull the vapor out of something awful and push you right inside of it. Or just cut the string and send you back out into the nothing. Then you're just potential again."

George was halfway out of his body, circling a drain.

"Nah, I won't do that," Joe said, and twirled his finger again. "Because you're not gonna tell. In fact, you're free to go."

George slumped out of the chair and stood on legs as sturdy as wet straw. He stumbled, walking backwards, toward the stairs.

"Hey! One more thing!" Joe barked.

George stopped with is hand on the bannister

Joe stood in the center of the room, the woman in crotchless overalls at his side.

"Gonna have a little celebration on Friday and I'd love to have some *real* company."

He placed his hand on the woman's slightly rounded belly.

"Probably goes against nature, but it's a miracle if you ask me. I'm thinkin' *Joe* if it's a boy."

HESITATION CUTS

There's something different about my wife. It's the pause before the smile, the confusion in her eyes, as if she is seeing me for the first time. Where do you go when you are not here with me, Anna?

This house is so empty with just us in it. No pitter patter of little feet, no bird-screech of wonder at a firefly trapped in a glass jar. And now you have become a specter, haunting your old paths with that smile that stops just before it touches your eyes. It is not a happy smile. It is a mockery.

It came to me in a dream, Anna. I dream a lot now, mostly of our life before. This dream was different. It felt real.

You were trapped inside of yourself, dear. Those tentative smiles that never quite coincided with the outside world were flickers of your former self, the YOU hidden within grayed flesh and cloud-white hair. You lay beside me in bed, facing the window as you always do. I watch the swell of your body as you inhale, snores like a mouse chewing a cracker.

I always loved to watch you sleep, Anna. In a marriage of fifty years there are few secrets, just these little slices of reality we tuck safely into our pockets, carry them around with us throughout the day. That was my secret. I watched you sleep, sometimes for an hour or more. In the dream I watch you sleep as well, a twitch of the shoulder hinting at your own conjured fantasy.

I reach across the bed to touch your back, something I do not do in life for fear of waking you. You shudder, not from the warmth of my palm but from something else. Your spine stiffens and your hand spider-crawls around your ribs, settling beneath your shoulder blade. Was it the whisper-thin fabric of your favorite nightgown, the tickle of a stray thread? It was a Christmas present from our granddaughter, Layla I think - bought with her own money she told us with a chest nearly bursting from pride.

You writhe, back arching as your fingers probe the spaces between your ribs. No, not the nightgown. Then I see it, a little bulge in the fabric. I know every inch of you, have loved every inch of you even as our inches, yours and mine, succumbed to the persistence of gravity. There is no bulge here. Or, there never was before.

I slide my palm over that familiar terrain hidden by a gauze of plum-colored cotton. I feel it, the bulge, hard as bone but flexible, relenting to the gentle pressure I place upon it. Time takes strange liberties with our bodies. It turned my knuckles into knots, softened your gums until your teeth fell out in your sleep. At night it sifts through your memories turning familiar faces into smudges, stealing names. But it does not create a growth in a span of hours...

I imagine it is your heartbeat against my palm at first, a little flutter barely noticed. But, no, it is something different. Something that should not be. I gasp, recalling my hand and holding it to my chest as if it was fire I touched and not your body. It disturbs the fabric of your nightgown from underneath, like a beetle crawling over your ribs. Your hand falls limply upon it as if trying to push it back in.

After seconds of holding my breath, I brush your hand aside. There it is, a periscope stretching the cotton. Your nightgown has a scooped back, and I snake my fingers within. There is little light in the room, a warped rectangle of milky orange on the floor. I squint and search for movement. My eyes are not so good, Anna, and my glasses never near when I need them. But I see something. Maybe. A strip of night hidden within the shadow of your shoulder blade.

The darkness matches the approximate area of the bulge in your nightgown. I inch my fingers closer, avoiding your skin so as not to wake you. Over the course of that brief journey my curiosity shifts into fear. It is difficult to control my hand, to prevent my twitching fingers from grazing you. And my knuckles block my view of the darkened strip.

I imagine it is a leech, suckling your flesh as its body turns to leather. Did I dream within my dream? Then I feel it, not a leech and not your skin, but warmth and moisture, like steam leaking from the seam between a boiling pot and its lid.

I woke and felt as if my belly was full of boiling leeches, such was the vividness of the dream. You snored like a single autumn leaf skittering over concrete. I rolled onto my side to face you, but there was little to see beyond a spider web of hair on your pillow. The comforter was pulled to your shoulder, nothing bulging beneath it, no moisture spreading. But it wasn't a dream, Anna. It was a message.

The next morning, we resume our wordless waltz, passing each other in silence like enemy ships without munitions. I do not know who is on the other end of the line listening to your gibberish, a very patient person or no one at all, I imagine.

"…just need a couple more days," you said before your words turned to mush. You noticed me watching from the dining room and hid the phone as if it was a bottle of brandy and you were a teenager again.

You sit in your favorite recliner, hands busy with a needlepoint you will never finish. Though so much of you is gone now this fragment remains, a glimpse of the way things were. I can almost hear our children squealing around your ankles like piglets. They are two things at once, now. Strange to think about it that way. They are both living, some far away, and ghosts - imprisoned in my mind as children.

I sit in my recliner across the room, tugging tufts of cotton free from the broken fabric. Did you do this, Anna? Did you slice up my chair as petty revenge for some offense I do not even remember?

"Anna?"

Your barn-owl eyes lock onto mine for a second. I believe, for a second, that I have you back, that your name spoken in the midnight stillness of our empty home cracked the facade of your sickness. The second stretches just as your smile does and the recognition bleeds from your eyes. Of course it would not be that easy.

You're still smiling as you place your project on your lap, left elbow aiming at the ceiling as you scratch your back, your shoulder blade. I inhale sharply, perhaps not loud enough for you to hear, as your hands resume their task and your smile melts into indifference.

Anna, my dear, Anna. You *are* trapped, just like those fireflies the kids used to torment. You're trapped inside of a body that has betrayed you. How long have you been trapped? Did it happen all at once or by degrees? We are ships Anna, but not enemies. You listed and sank so quietly, a blade in water, and now this husk sits in your chair.

I have to free you, Anna. We only have a few years left if we're lucky. And I won't spend them with an impostor.

NIGHT TAKES ITS TIME, OR MAYBE IT'S JUST THE SEASON. In my old age I find it endlessly surprising how easily seasons merge and overlap, the familiar touchstones of Christmas or the Fourth of July stripped of meaning without our little piglets to delight in them. I stand in the cold bathroom struggling to read the label of the pill bottle. There is a small army of them between our sinks. I confess I mostly forget what they are intended to cure or keep at bay. Arthritis, a bad heart, a half dozen more things some physician told me about a decade ago. The words are too small for my old eyes, side effects and instructions like fuzzy little caterpillars wiggling on the label. I think I remember which ones made me sleepy.

I dump a few into my hand and tiptoe on cat's paws to the bedroom door. The TV is on and there are no sounds of movement. Back in the bathroom, I grind the pills into dust, sweep the dust into an empty bottle, then palm it.

And now I wait for the right moment.

YOU ARE NODDING IN YOUR CHAIR, NOT IN AGREEMENT WITH whatever TV judge show you are half-watching, but in defiance of the sleep attempting to claim you. We both nap a lot now, preparing for the big sleep to come I suppose. Hopefully I can steal a few more good years with you before then.

My feet morph into cat's paws again as I pad to your chair and pluck your iced tea from the tray, a few melted cubes rattling the glass. Your eyes pop open and lock onto mine. I feel like a burglar, Anna, a kid with his hand in the cookie jar. Your lips part but the words come out watery, and you angle your shoulder away from me as if I might strike you. As if I have ever done so in our fifty plus years.

In that moment you are a stranger to me. Your face melts into a mask, skin pooling where it shouldn't, eyes like ice marbles suspended in a red-threaded spiderweb.

Anna, I don't even recognize you when you're like this. I don't even recognize you. And so I turn and shuffle away, no longer padding on cat's paws. It's too tough on my knees, anyway.

Your watery words lap at my back as I reach the kitchen, but you do not follow me. With an ear aimed at the living room I shake a bit of the powder onto the ice cubes, then fill the cup with more ice and tea. An extra packet of sugar just to be sure and I stir the ice with my finger. I mean to wipe the tea onto my robe and instead streak it across my naked belly. For a moment the world's edges seem to sharpen. The TV judge's voice crackles in the living room.

"What?"

Where is my robe? I think I took a shower, yes. I took a shower and then...but my hair is not wet. I did not take a shower. I take showers at night. Always have. For a moment in that crisp world with the obnoxious, tired judge I see my pale legs, thighs a road map of blue veins, pubic hair like a forgotten bird's nest above them.

"Where is..."

The judge's voice dives underwater, and the world softens, the edges nice and safe now. I blink and find I *am* wearing my robe. How strange that was.

I shuffle back into the living room, spill a little tea on the way. It splashes cold on my toes. You grip the armrests of your chair as if you are afraid there are rockets strapped to the back of it and you might blast off at any moment. I smile so widely it hurts my cheeks as I place your iced tea back on the tray. You smile back, something familiar blossoming in your eyes. I nod as gibberish spills out of your mouth and claim my seat.

I do not watch you from the corner of my eye, Anna. I listen to the clink of the ice cubes striking glass. You drink small sips. It takes a while. But within fifteen minutes you are slumped and snoring, and I am on my way back upstairs.

The little box of shaving razors is hidden behind a small stack of cloth diapers we stored for a grandbaby who must be approaching middle school by now. Funny what I remember and what slips away. I knew the razors would be there despite not touching them for a decade, but if you asked me the grandchild's name it would have been a struggle. There were three or four babies around the same time and, to be honest, they all kind of looked the same.

I slide the cardboard top off the carton and the razors rattle like sleet tinkling on a window.

"Rats," I mutter, plucking a rust-spotted razor from the box. Moisture got in somehow and each of the razors is similarly corrupted. No matter. I only need the blade to be sharp.

I can hear your snores in the spaces between my steps as I descend the stairs, razor held away from me in case I take a tumble. It has happened before. My hip reminds me when it rains.

Look at you, Anna. Who carved those lines in your face, turned your plump cheeks into wrinkled jowls? Something crueler than nature, has to be. The same something that burrowed into your mind at night and made a mess of your memories. But I will liberate you. I am only sorry it took me so long to understand.

I place the razor next to the sweating glass of tea and gently turn your body. You snore louder, sleep deeper. Good. The last thing I want is to hurt you, Anna, even though it is no longer *you*. And this will be an exploratory mission, not the real thing I imagine. I tug the sleeve of your house dress below your shoulder, bone white and freckled with a spray of peach pepper flakes.

Where to begin? The dream had a suggestion, but now that I see it, your shoulder blade, I wonder. Are you swimming inside of yourself? You need to be able to see the light when I cut. I don't want to cut more than once. There are marks here, faded pink lines like cat scratches, a dozen or more of them. I think this is right. I think you have tried to escape here before.

Just a test, not the real thing. I swallow hard, the lump in my throat like a cold river rock. I nearly reach for the tea, but my hand slides past it and I retrieve the razor.

My fingers are trembling now, the blade like a chink of ice. How can I do this, Anna? We have been through so much together, so many years and now I stand beside you with a razor hovering above your skin. As if in response you moan in your sleep, the *real* you, Anna. The you imprisoned within this graying old dough.

Just a test, Anna, a quick cut to see if what has taken over you can sleep through it. My fingers do not stop shaking until the corner of the blade touches your skin, not piercing it, just resting as I gather my nerves.

"It's okay," I whisper as your snores persist.

The blade glistens. My fingers are wet.

I shake my head and sweat sprinkles the chair and your body. A determined drop of it twitches on the tip of my nose.

"Oh…"

There is a line of red above the razor, just a thin thread. I must have pulled it inadvertently. Blood breeches the surface of your skin, overflows it just a little. It was not even where I intended to cut, not that I had made my mind up about that. You shudder, the razor cuts in a jagged line, deeper this time. I did not mean to do that either. More blood, darker.

"Oh no," I say.

I am not prepared for this. A rivulet courses in the shallow gulley between your ribs. You moan again, louder. The slash is about the length of my thumb, the blood gurgling slowly from it.

DING

The razor blade slips from my grasp and lands on the narrow red stream. It floats an inch or two and then adheres to your skin.

The doorbell, were you expecting someone? I confess I have always left our daily schedule to you and never considered changing that arrangement even as…

Even as you…

Even…

Even as you…

There is a barrier between me and the completion of the thought. For a moment I forget my purpose, forget why I loom over your bleeding back, my thumb a wet cherry above the red smudge beside your shoulder blade.

DING

The door. I shuffle toward it, my thoughts a kaleidoscope, fragments of a dream, slivers of intention out of focus.

"Coming!" I mumble, spittle falling out of my mouth and landing on my belly.

My belly. I stop in the dining room and catch a glimpse of a ghost in the glass of the grandfather clock, a ghost or something like it. It is a haggard thing, beard like dirty snow, wild wisps of hair clinging to a gray, liver-spotted dome. He stares back at me, hunched, caught in the act. Of what I do not know. Below his wrinkled paunch of a belly is his member, which looks like a sprig of ginger forgotten in the back of the pantry.

"Hey!" I say, and his mouth opens in concert.

I paw at my belly, and he does the same.

But I was wearing a robe. I-I've been through this before. I took a shower…no, I did not take a shower. I put the robe on when…

I hear voices, faint, at the front door. That is where I am headed. The reflection of me is wearing his robe again, and I feel its warmth, the stiff but comfortable cotton.

"Coming!" I say, more spit falling out of my mouth.

I peer through the peephole, but my eyes are not so good and my glasses never near when I need them. Two people on the porch, that's about the best I can do.

I open the door part way and one, a boy of maybe fifteen, begins to speak. I can't hear him so well. He speaks so softly but I nod my head anyway as he points to the lawnmower on the sidewalk and then makes a few more motions with his hands. I open the door fully and he stops speaking.

He takes a step backward as I take one forward. A boy on the sidewalk, his little brother maybe, covers his mouth with his hand. The boy in front of me is descending the stairs, palms displayed as if I am a rabid dog. He speaks so softly, why can't he speak louder? I take another step forward and he turns to run, slipping over his untied shoelaces.

They've left the lawnmower. I shout at their backs that they've left the lawnmower. But they are jackrabbit fast and neither breaks stride as they disappear around the corner of the street.

"Ohh…"

Anna, I forgot you. I amble inside, shutting the door and sliding across the tiles as if my feet are skis.

"Ohhh…" you call again from the living room.

I am coming Anna; bad hip be damned.

You are where I left you, tilted to the side in your chair, your bare shoulder exposed. Blood glistens on your back as you moan again.

"Anna!"

I rush to your side as best I am able.

Who hurt you?

Your hand numbly crawls over your shoulder, fingers dangling like bait worms above the streak of blood.

The razor is glued to your back and I remember now. I remember who did this to you. Who did this *for* you. I peel the razor free and place it in my…

"Ouch!"

A sharp pain below my hip, a dark snail-trail of blood oozing. My robe is gone again. Must have come loose as I shuffled back from the front door. No time to think about it now. I drop the blade and nudge it under your chair with my toe then pivot and stagger back toward the kitchen to the sound of your hand slapping at your back.

Where did you put the paper towels, Anna? You are always moving things in this house. Everything is a blur, and my glasses are never near when I need them. The blood on my thigh trickles past the knee where the leg hair slows its descent.

"Ooohhh…"

Goddammit where are the paper towels?

I snatch a dish rag from the oven handle and wipe the blood off my thigh. It smears around my knee, the leg hairs pasting to my skin.

"Ooohhh…"

I hear you, Anna. I am coming. Just can't have you question why my leg is all bloody. Can't have whatever has imprisoned you question it. That's what this is all about, isn't it? Something about a dream…about how you were trapped inside of yourself, right? I catch a glimpse of the ghost in the grandfather clock, naked again, as I return to the living room. Don't have time to think about him now.

Your head sways as if your neck is made of putty. You are trying to sit up but one hand is still straining to reach the cut on your back. It no longer bleeds, but you must feel it through the drugs. I place a hand on your shoulder and your whole body jolts. I press the dish rag to your wound and you seethe, eyes wide but unfocused.

"S'okay, Anna," I say, or something like it.

Your right hand crawls toward the dish rag like a house cat stalking prey.

"S'okay," I say.

My mind is racing, trying to think of a way to explain the cut on your back. But then you do the most wonderful thing, Anna. I think it is the *real* you clawing to the surface for just a moment. You sit up, blinking, and hold out your hand. Something glints in the afternoon light seeping through the gaps in the blinds. I squint to see. I don't see so good, and my glasses are never near when I need them.

It's a needle. And your eyes swell with gratitude as I wipe the drying blood off your back. You, the real you, convinces whatever controls your mind that it was your own fault. You fell asleep with the needle in your hand and accidentally cut yourself. You do this for me. You have given me another chance to free you. I just need to summon the courage to cut deeper.

IT IS NIGHT NOW AND YOU ARE ASLEEP BESIDE ME. THE WORLD beyond our window is quiet, no crickets or cars, nothing rising above the sound of your breaths, which pass between whispers and snores. The bandage on your back glows in the darkness of our room, a rectangle of moonlight. Feathers leak from gashes in my pillow and they feel like moth's wings against my cheek. I flip it over, but the other side is similarly damaged.

A breath, a snore. Your body swells and deflates and my eyes rest upon the bandage. It's a bit of a blur, and my glasses are never near when I need them. The razor blade is warm in my hand, slick with sweat. I just need a small sign, Anna, a nudge in the right direction. I don't think I can cut you there again, and the bandage would be too cumbersome to remove.

I search the terrain of your back, the lighter flesh blending into the plum that presents as black in the darkness. I need you to move, Anna, find a new place to surface and I will free you.

I lick my lips and my tongue sticks there a moment they are so dry.

A breath and a snore and nothing more. I would wait a lifetime to free you, but I am afraid there is not much left for me in this one. I swap the razor for the pill bottle hidden in my nightstand and creep on cat's paws again. Down the stairs, hip hurts – must be rain coming.

You drink half of whatever that God-awful protein stuff is at night and half in the morning. I know this like I knew the razors were behind the cloth diapers. One of your talk show ladies promoted it a while back and I've been living with the smell of it on your breath ever since. Even your *change* hasn't altered this habit. It is a part of you, like the needlepoint, like your thoughtless smiles.

Blue and white bottle, top shelf as always. I empty the rest of the powder and give the bottle a good shake, take the tiniest sip to test it. It *is* God-awful, but still tastes like a protein drink.

In bed beside you, snoring like you always have. I wonder about this mixture, these flashes of *you* amid the changes. If I hadn't been paying attention, Anna, to you all these years I might have thought I was mistaken. I might dismiss your feeble attempts to communicate as aging, your inability to smile convincingly as the pooled weariness of a long life. It is hard to smile, isn't it? With the light at your back and so much darkness ahead. Is my smile convincing?

I *have* been paying attention. I did not need a dream to tell me you were trapped. I just needed to know how to fix you.

I DREAM OF YOU, NOT IN AN ENDEARING WAY. NO HONEY-colored recollection of a Saturday morning on the porch, bumblebees with their black and yellow sweaters hovering around your hips as you water your tomatoes. No soundtrack of piglets in the yard, shoes slick with dew as they chase each other with sticks. Rusty, our favorite mutt slicing through the grass mashing dandelions into paste. Instead, I dream we are together, in darkness. It is warm, womb-like. When you speak to me here, I understand your words and not just because we are close but because we are connected. You speak of silent suffering, how fearful you are of the dark, how I can bring light into your world again.

We kiss, as we have not done for many years. I pull away, my tongue throbbing as if a tiny heart is lodged in its tip. Blood fills my cheeks, seeps past my lips.

"Anna…" I say.

But you have swum away to some other darkened corner.

I pull the razor from between my lips, press it against the warm thickness of my enclosure, and cut. The key, Anna, you gave it to me.

I STARE AT THE WINDOW, MORNING LIGHT BREAKING AGAINST the curtains with little penetrating. Where am I? It is just me and the window for a minute, a minute that stretches. I have many thoughts in my mind, but they are hazy, wrapped in fog. They flit past showing shapes and colors but refusing to collect into something recognizable.

The light. The window. A taste in my mouth, like saltwater but not quite. My tongue traces the ridges of my gums. Shapes and colors. The light.

A light, a light after the darkness. A shape coalesces, its colors muted by shadows. Anna pulling her lips away from mine, metal on my tongue.

Anna.

I call your name, try to, anyway. Your side of the bed is tidy, comforter pulled tight and tucked beneath the mattress. My heart thunders with the knowledge of what I must do.

"What?"

The nightstand drawer is open. I fumble with the lamp's switch. It's like trying to pinch a tick that keeps moving.

I did not hide the razor blade. It should be right on top, glinting lamplight back at me. I also did not leave the drawer open, which means…

I am not so quick now, not so nimble, and so I scramble to the bathroom as if my right and left leg were swapped in the night. The pill bottles are there, your brush with the snarls of hair like bleached moss. But where are the razors?

Where are the razors? Where did I put that little box? My blood is cold like mud after a November storm. Which did you find first, Anna? The box of razors or the one in my nightstand? The box I imagine. Yesterday I… we…after the incident I…

Here comes the fog again, blunting the edges of my thoughts, softening my memories of yesterday. I sit on the edge of the tub. It is cold, sends a ripple of goosebumps across my thighs. I sit and think – try to think. I think about thinking. I imagine this is what life is like for you, Anna. How terrifying to lose yourself.

THWACK

The sound is like an old pumpkin dropped on concrete. I follow it, through the bedroom and down the stairs. Hip hurts, must be rain coming. In the wake of that sound there is no other, no talk show ladies or angry judges, just the ticking of the grandfather clock with the ghost in the glass.

"Anna?"

The word is clear in my head but comes out as something different, as if my tongue was replaced by a dollop of pudding. I hear something, not above the ticking clock but between the ticks, a voice, a small one.

"Anna?"

It is not your voice. It sounds like something that would come out of a toy.

"Anna…"

You are dressed as if the very next thing you were going to do was leave. You have a kerchief around your hair, knotted beneath your chin. There is a small travel bag on the kitchen island, an empty bottle of protein drink beside it. Why are you sleeping on the floor, Anna?

Mom! Mom!

The voice reminds me of our granddaughter's doll, Josie I think. No, that was the doll, not the child.

"Anna?"

It feels like a cord is snipped within me, one that gave strength to my legs and arms. It is a gift, Anna. You have given me a gift, an opportunity to finish what I started. I take the phone from your hand and press it to my ear.

Mom! What happened! Mom, I'm coming over right now.

The words lose shape and mean nothing to me. I hang up the phone and leave it on the tiles. It rings immediately. The sight of the protein drink shines a light on my memories, cutting through the haze. You must have known, my dear, even as the *other* you dug through my nightstand and hid the razors the *real* you knew. There is a little stream of blood leaking from your nose and your eyes are half-open. Your breaths are automatic, short and shallow.

The razors, where did you hide them? I peek into your travel bag, but you would not be that obvious, would you? A knife would suffice, but there are none on the countertops. I open the knife drawer but find only spatulas. You are always moving things, Anna. I understand it is not you but some indefinable *other*, but I don't have time to consider these things.

I need to cut. I need to cut but have no knife. The *other* hid the razors and I have no knife.

Your eyelid flutters and the blood seeping from your nostrils is like sap crawling down the trunk of a tree. No knife and I need to cut.

Then I recall where this all began, not my suspicions about your condition but the knowledge to liberate you. The dream, the glimpse of some shadowed seam on your back. I drag you to the center of the kitchen and roll you onto your belly. There is a little puff in the fabric above your shoulder blade, the bandage from yesterday. Maybe…maybe I can't make a new cut. Maybe I can use the old one.

I am sorry for this part, love. Can't be concerned about modesty now. I strip your blouse, buttons pinging across the tiles like BBs. Your arms are ragdoll loose but still difficult to free from the sleeves. And there it is, the bandage, a little slice of brown where the blood dried. I straddle you, then rip it off and the scab breaks, blood cresting and overflowing the wound.

The phone rings again and I feel your body tense for half a second, in response or in the grip of a dream I don't know. Can't be polite now, Anna. I'm so sorry it came to this. You didn't choose your affliction like I didn't choose for my teeth to fall out in my sleep.

No, that was you, I think.

I carve through the leftover scab grit. It is not a deep cut, but the skin is thin here. I press the pad of my finger into the wound, wiggle it to create more space. In my mind it's easy, just get a hook inside and pull. The reality of it is not easy, especially the getting inside part. I hover my face over the wound. It's longer now but no deeper. Are you in there? I wish you would show yourself to me.

The skin tore north and south but not much. I don't have the time to do it this way, Anna, *we* don't.

Where are the razors? They must be around somewhere, the trash can maybe. Where is the trash can? You are always moving things, Anna. Maybe in your needlepoint kit? I shuffle through the dining room past the carved up recliner in the living room. Your needlepoint kit is tidy, Anna, but I can't make sense of it without my glasses and they're never near when I need them. The razors, where did you hide…

My toe touches something cold and smooth. I might not have noticed, but it is also sharp. I kneel, joints popping like miles-off fireworks, and pull the razor from under the recliner. Anna, you left this for me. How did you know I would find it? Tears brim. I am so close to having you back.

NO NEED TO BE DELICATE NOW. NO NEED FOR A STRAIGHT line, just has to be deep. I press the edge of the razor to the right of the cut already there, not on purpose, just where my shakes lead me. It sinks into your skin and red blossoms to either side. I pull it out. I swallow. You moan and I don't know if I can do this. I press the razor to your skin again, pierce and drag, but my fingers are disconnected from my will. Now there are three wounds on your back, one scabbing over again and two new additions, as if you were scratched by a cat with three different sized claws, faded scars mingled with fresh cuts.

The phone rings. You moan. I am running out of time. *You are not doing this **to** her. You are doing it **for** her.*

It makes sense, but it doesn't stop my hand from shaking. I press the razor again, and a new red bulb emerges from your skin.

I am doing this **for** you.

I close my eyes and pull, push deeper and pull harder. You stiffen beneath me, and I push harder, pull harder. It feels like miles but is probably only inches. I pull until the razor touches the fabric of your pants. I can't look, Anna. I can't look at what I've done. I made it bright for you. Can't you see the light?

My hand falls into a puddle, fingers probe the seam of your skin. Do you see my fingers, Anna? It's warm, wet, and tougher than I would have guessed. What am I touching? I peak but see only red up to my wrist. Grab my hand, Anna.

The phone rings again. Your body is rigid beneath me. Please take my hand, Anna. Yes, we only have a few good years left, but I would rather a single good afternoon with the *real* you than a lifetime sitting across the room from an impostor.

Please take my hand, Anna. I push deeper, two hands inside now. Bone and organs, muscle and tendons repelling then relenting. They feel like fingers, like your hand reaching for mine, but it passes.

I sob. I am up to my elbows now. My knees are wet, and the room smells like a pail of old, rusty nails. A steady moan from your lips, but your body relaxes beneath me, and the moan passes into a whisper.

I SIT IN YOUR RECLINER. IT SMELLS LIKE YOU HERE, AND that's a good smell. Your unfinished needlepoint is on the tray to the right. I squint to read it. I don't see so good, and my glasses are never near when I need them. The letters come in and out of focus.

"H-h-appy…Ann…Anna…v-very s-sorry?"

I think that's what it says. Another message from you I do not understand. The phone keeps ringing, but I won't go back in that room, not while that impostor is still in there, floating on the red tiles.

Hip hurts, might be rain, but through the window I see only blue.

I sit up. There is no rain. And you were not where you showed me you would be.

I intend to remove my robe but find that has already happened. I press my hip with a knuckle. The muscles twitch in response.

The muscles or something else. Some*one* else.

You. You were not where the dream showed me.

My hip aches and there is no rain coming.

From here I can see the ghost in the grandfather clock. He holds up a razor blade and I show him mine. We nod to each other.

A little cut to begin. Just need to let the light in, Anna.

3

THE BYSTANDER

My mother said I came out incomplete, that the best parts of me dribbled down her leg when my father was finished. This was meant to hurt me, I think. I'm not skilled at understanding interactions like that. I nodded, waited for her to say more, but instead she took a long drink from the bottle of gin she'd been nursing for a few hours. I think that was supposed to hurt me as well.

I understand physical pain just fine. I've been brought to my knees from a stubbed toe more than once. It's that other interpretation of pain, the one you can't see, that never really resonated.

"Don't you love me?" Mom asked.

I peeked around my hand, held in front of my face so I wouldn't see her breasts floating on top of the pink water. She smiled, eyes swinging lazily between me and her arm as if wanting me to notice it. The blood wasn't flowing as quickly now. I almost told her she didn't cut deep enough but it felt like one of those things she would get mad at me for.

"Yes, Mom."

I did. That wasn't a lie. I loved my mom.

She smiled.

The tendons in my shoulder felt like warm string cheese, so I dropped my hand. I blurred my vision so Mom's breasts were out of focus, but even fuzzy and glimpsed peripherally, warmth pooled below my bellybutton.

"Then why don't you stop me?" she asked, gesturing at the razorblade on the porcelain next to her ear.

I swallowed. I usually messed these moments up, said the wrong thing. Mom wanted to kill herself. She said so more times than I could count. Other than telling me my father was only good for his money that was probably the most common phrase uttered in our house. I understood she wanted to die. I understood when she did die there would be no more Mom. I would have to live with Uncle Dale because Dad said I wasn't allowed around his real family.

"Mom?"

She sat up in the tub a bit, breasts creeping back into view.

"Yes?"

"Will I have to change schools?"

She frowned, hope draining from her eyes, "What?"

"I really like the lunches at my school, and I don't know if I would like them as much at another school if you kill yourself and I have to move in with Uncle Dale."

"Lunches?"

I nodded, "The tater tots are the best."

She sank into the water until it touched the bottom of her chin.

"Do…do you *want* me to die?"

"No."

"But you won't stop me?"

"No."

She took a deep breath.

"Can you leave, please?"

I stood, took a step toward the door, but hesitated there, "Mom?"

"Yes?"

"Do you know if the new school will have tater tots?"

GARY 2 IS ALMOST READY. HE'S ASLEEP AT THE MOMENT, THE cat he named Mr. Gray like fresh from the dryer laundry between his legs. It's kind of funny he named the cat Mr. Gray when his name is Gary 2. They're almost the same. Maybe he hasn't made the connection.

I named him Gary 2 because when I made it back to the Gs I couldn't think of another name that started with G. (Later I thought of George, but he didn't look like a George) It's like how they used to name hurricanes, I think. That's probably where I got the idea. I'll admit, I skipped over the X. All X names are really Z names anyway.

I've learned so much from Gary 2. We've been through a lot together. Gary 2 doesn't know he is almost ready, probably thinks this is just what his life is now. Considering what he endured in the past year or so the prospect might be comforting.

He was scarecrow-thin the day I picked him up. A junkie, obviously, which is not my first choice among subjects, but they're easy pickings.

My dad came around more after his wife divorced him. Uncle Dale spilled the beans about Dad's other family after Mom died. I think Dad was okay with it as he was ready for something new.

It was through my dad I learned if you present a certain image to the world, you can get away with pretty much anything. It isn't *wealthy*, either. Many people make that mistake. Do you think an addict or runaway pregnant teenager would get into a Porsche? No. I would have my hackles raised as well. Surprisingly, I've had the most success with my pickup truck. It's modern but not new, comfortable but not top-of-the-line. Maybe it reminds people of their own fathers or grandpas.

There was nothing special about Gary 2 when I found him off Grand Street, other than he was alone. He wore more layers than the weather required and rubbed his hands together either to keep them busy or warm. I told him I would get him some clean needles and food, said he could use my shower. Though I didn't have any drugs for him I would drop him off on Grand Street with money to carry him through the weekend. That was enough, the hope of another fix more than the prospect of a meal or shower.

There he is now, sleeping with Mr. Gray flipping his tail in the midst of a dream. I am anxious to push Gary 2 across the finish line, but not so anxious I need to wake him unnecessarily. I want the realization to be organic. I want him to put the puzzle pieces together with no outside influence. It's what he's here for after all.

While I wait for him to wake, I access the Gary 2 file with all my favorite moments. It's a big file. He's been here longer than any subject by a margin of six months. Junkies present a specific challenge; in that it is difficult to predict what combination of drugs and in what amount will incapacitate them without killing them. Most of the downtown junkies are on heroin, and I have a pretty reliable cocktail for them, but I've been wrong before.

On the day I found him, Gary 2 was obviously on heroin and the cocktail left him draped over the kitchen island before it was half consumed.

There are four cameras in Gary 2's room. The ceiling-mounted camera offers an overall view but is blurry in the corners. Another behind Gary 2's bed is trained on the door I use to enter and exit. A third covers the bathroom area. Gary 2 woke an hour-and-a-half after his cocktail. I guess he needed the sleep. In the recording, he starts pawing at the collar around his neck. The fourth camera is zoomed on Gary 2's face, though it is actually programmed to follow the sensor in his collar. This is my favorite view. He hasn't blinked for over a minute. What's going on in that mushy brain of yours, Gary 2?

He jolts as I enter the room, eyebrows dancing between fear and hope. Here he is, collared, a chain fastened to the hasp on the back of the collar which vanishes into the floor, and he still smiles when he recognizes me. He thinks I am here to save him. Must be the plaid shirt, maybe the slight paunch of my belly. I don't look like someone who would do this. That's fair. He doesn't look like someone who would survive as long as he has.

"Your name is Gary 2," I tell him.

"What? My n-name is-"

"Your name is Gary 2."

He slips a finger inside the collar and tugs. I pluck the remote from my pocket and show it to him. I flip the switch and the chain retracts, plastering Gary 2 to the bed, cutting off his air as the gears begin to squeak at the resistance. He yelps and I flip the switch to reverse the chain, giving him a little slack. Each time I demonstrate the remote for a subject I am reminded of Oprah.

Now, you're going to conjure a mental image of Oprah, and I would advise you to examine your prejudices. When I got to the Os it was the first name I thought of. I made the mistake of leaving the remote in my front pocket as I went about my day, and I guess the switch flipped inadvertently. I hadn't even checked the monitor when I entered the room with lunch (turkey sandwiches), so it was quite a surprise. Her roommate was just as surprised. He cried while cleaning Oprah's hair and blood out of the gears of the contraption, which was very peculiar as, to my knowledge, he didn't even know her.

But he did get an extra turkey sandwich for lunch, so that's something.

"Wh-what is this? Why am I here?" Gary 2 asks.

He doesn't perceive me as a threat yet.

"Whatever happens, just behave as you normally would. You don't need to perform," I say, indicating the cameras in the room. "It won't change anything."

"I don't understand."

"That's fine," I say, turning to leave.

"Wait!"

I stop, hand on the doorknob.

"What about my fix?"

For all the problems they present, junkies are endlessly fascinating. Their thoughts always travel in the same direction, even when they're cleaning Oprah's flesh and gray matter from the teeth of a gear the size of an eighteen-wheeler's hubcap.

I check the live feed. Gary 2 stretches his twig arms over his head. He calls for Mr. Gray, watches the doggie door I added to the main door, but the cat is no longer in the room. Mr. Gray's food and water dishes are in the kitchen. I do not interact with the cat beyond filling its dishes. It is not my cat after all.

Gary 2 inspects the floor. He swallows, Adam's Apple like a baby's fist trapped in his throat. He looks at the camera, expression blank but his eyes are screaming. Gary 2 has not eaten in three days. His belief this is an oversight is buckling. We have a history with food, and as Gary 2 considers the emptiness of his belly I open another file.

It was Gary 2's fourth day. The first night was rough for him. The withdrawals hit him hard right about the time the pizza delivery showed up. I always order pizza on junkie-withdrawal days. It's the perfect food because if I don't finish the whole pie I don't have to rush to the refrigerator to preserve it. I usually want another slice before bed, anyway.

Gary 2 always vomited in the blue bucket, which I appreciated because some of his predecessors acted like they were auditioning for The Exorcist 4 (or did they already make that one?). Junkie puke is among the worst things I have smelled. Mom's body is still probably number one, but not by a lot. After I added the drain to the floor it wasn't so bad, just hose 'em off like Mom used to spray the cat turds off our driveway. They were strays. Mom said I couldn't be trusted with animals.

Gary 2 hadn't kept anything down for days and the fog in his brain was beginning to lift. His body's primal needs surpassed the ache of withdrawal. He prodded his ribs and smacked his waxy lips, drank all the water I provided.

I enter the room, the tray wobbly as the bowl slides back and forth. The camera doesn't capture my face well, which is good because I tend to bite my lip when concentrating and it looks a little silly. In another view Gary 2 sits up. He is no longer confused about my role in his captivity. He hides behind skeleton fingers, eyes swollen grapes held together by throbbing capillaries. I place the tray on the floor, nod, and walk away. Gary 2 watches the door for a minute. Then he worms across the bed, certain he won't have enough slack to reach the tray. He does reach it, however.

There are so many expressions on his face, eyebrows arching and collapsing, lips undulating offering glimpses of gray gums and candy corn teeth. He looks toward the camera and back to the bowl, then places it on the floor, not with violence as some before. Confusion, maybe?

He might suspect I was attempting to poison him. What a waste of effort that would be, to kidnap someone, hold them hostage for days only to poison their food.

Gary 2 stirs the spaghetti, which is just noodles and room temperature, extra chunky pasta sauce. I used to put more effort into the meals, but the subjects were unreliable with their feedback, only telling me what I wanted to hear (if still able to speak). He twirls the tiniest bite and grazes his tongue past it, recoiling at once. Sigh, there goes my Michelin star. Hand on belly, he scrapes a bit off with his teeth. He chews, casts a sideways glance at the camera, and chews some more.

He licks his lips, twirls again, then takes a big bite. His cheeks swell like a water balloon. He chews. Once. Twice. Then he shudders, sits upright, glances at the camera. He opens his mouth, and pulverized noodles slide past his lips, the cartoon red of the sauce mingled with a darker crimson. He pinches a shard of glass, holds it under the lamp, then looks back at the bowl. He stirs, blood dangling from his lips in twisting ribbons.

What is that expression on your face, Gary 2? What do you feel? Betrayed? You didn't even know me. Sad? Angry? Help me understand. Gary 2 places the bowl on the tray, nudges it under the neighboring bed, then zombie-walks to the bathroom sink where he spits pink water in the sink until it turns clear.

"WHAT DO YOU MEAN SHE'S DEAD, AVERY?"

I held my nose as I peeked inside the bathroom. The water had drained from the tub, and I could only see a hemisphere of her shoulder. Still dead. Extra dead, actually. The skin looked like bread dough rolled in cigarette ash.

"She killed herself, Uncle Dale, just like she wanted. Remember how she always said that?"

"Avery, what-this doesn't make sense. What are you saying? Have you checked to make sure she's not breathing?"

"I checked the first day. She wasn't breathing then."

"What do you mean the first day? When did this…"

"Last week."

"She killed herself last week?!"

Uncle Dale's concern was slipping into anger.

"Yeah, but she wanted to. She told me all the time and…"

"Avery, why are you…why are you just telling me now, I c-could've saved…"

I cleared my throat, "No, she did a really good job, went all the way to the bone. Not like the other times."

"But why didn't you call?" he sobbed.

"Well, um, Friday is tater tots day at school and…"

WHAT DID I FEEL WATCHING GARY 2 EAT ROOM TEMPERATURE spaghetti and glass shards? More importantly, what *should* I have felt? Uncle Dale was inconsolable when he arrived, though he and Mom were only birthday-phone call-close. He punched holes in the walls and kept gripping me by the shoulders, tears in his eyes and asking me to tell him how it happened.

Mom died because she wanted to. Why punch holes in the wall over that? Gary 2 more than likely did not want to eat a spaghetti with glass shards in it, but my reaction to witnessing it was the same.

It shouldn't have been. I know that even if I don't understand it. Mom said I was incomplete. If I am today, it is not for lack of trying.

Back on the live feed, Gary 2 crouches to check beneath the unoccupied bed across from his. No, there is no food under the bed, Gary 2. This isn't an Easter egg hunt; it's a make Avery whole hunt. He sits on the bed, two hands on his stomach now, and watches the doggie door. Do you still call it a doggie door if it's only a cat using it?

Gary 2 hasn't had a roommate in a while. The last one nearly broke him, I think. I navigate to my Gary 2 and Rita file, skip past their first couple of days together. Gary 2 was so helpful pushing her through withdrawals. He held her hair when she puked, told her not to trust anything I fed her the first few days. In fact, Gary 2 shared his food with her, even inspected it for glass first.

They were becoming friends. I introduced television to the dynamic, one of those fatbacks the teachers used to wheel in to play Bill Nye the Science Guy. Gary 2 mostly let Rita pick. I improved the quality of the food, switched the toilet paper to three-ply. Things were going well for them. Rita sometimes watched TV from Gary 2's bed. He pretended to watch, to be interested in the TV judge shows she favored, but mostly he looked at her. He sought moments for them to touch, picking lint off her top, counting and comparing track marks.

Gary 2 drapes an arm over Rita's shoulder when I enter. He is her protector now. I tell Rita to come with me and show her the remote to remind her she does not have a choice in the matter. She does. I provide enough slack for her to follow me through the door. There is no camera here, but I remember the interaction.

"What is this?" she asks, hands like little mallets at her side.

"Almond Joy. It's coconut with almonds. I buy all I can because it seems like one of those candies no one eats except for me, and I worry they're going to go out of business."

"No thank you," she sneers.

I show her the remote and she puts out her hand.

"Don't tell Gary 2. I didn't bring one for him. Eat it and give me the wrapper."

She does. There was no expression on her face, but my guess is she doesn't prefer coconut in her chocolate. I take the wrapper and tell her, "Remember, Rita, don't tell Gary 2. I'm listening."

Gary 2 peppers her with questions, which she deflects, "He said not to tell you."

He reclaims the remote, spreads out on the bed so she can't join him. For dinner that evening (ham sandwiches with kettle chips) I include a stick of spearmint gum for each of them. Inside the wrapper of Gary 2's gum I wrote:

Check toilet tank after Rita is asleep. Don't tell her. I'm listening.

I do dose their food and beverages occasionally. Just enough to so they will not wake if I enter the room. The night before I hid a "junkie kit" inside the tank of the toilet. I included everything Gary 2 would need for his fix except for the heroin. I also included a boxcutter and another note.

Made Rita swallow sixteen baggies of heroin.

Gary 2 sits on the bed, back to Rita who was asleep. He reads the note for maybe the fiftieth time, examines the supplies again. He doesn't look at the cameras, seems to have forgotten where he is. Remember what I said about a junkie's thoughts? It goes for recovering junkies as well.

"Hey!" he hisses.

She wakes after the seventh attempt.

He shows her the kit and the note.

"Just throw it up. W-we can use the bucket," Gary 2 says.

He's rubbing his hands together.

"Wh-what? No. He didn't give me heroin. He gave me a fucking nasty candy bar."

(I was right about the coconuts)

"Don't lie to me. Why w-would he g-give you candy? That doesn't make sense."

"I don't know why! He made me eat it in front of him then told me not to tell you."

"You're lying."

"Why would I lie about that?"

It's then Rita notices the boxcutter. Gary 2 has a death grip on it.

"Then throw up and prove it," Gary 2 says, leaning forward.

She refuses.

The argument persists for thirty minutes. At the end of it, Gary 2 is standing over an eviscerated corpse, sobbing, hands thick with Rita's blood. There is no heroin. He was very thorough in his search.

During her conversations with Gary 2 Rita mentioned she never wanted to be a mother, that she would be terrible at it. Well, bullet dodged on that one, but it was a hell of a way to find out.

MR. GRAY IS ASLEEP ON GARY 2'S BED. HIS BELLY IS EXTRA full. Gary 2 sniffs the tuna-scented air around the cat and cradles his stomach again. Mr. Gray is his only friend in the whole world, probably the sole reason he hasn't drowned himself in the toilet. But a thought has invaded Gary 2's mind. He eases off the bed, careful not to wake the sleeping puff ball. There are tears in his eyes as he shuffles to the toilet. He checks the tank.

No. Not this time. You have the right idea, though.

He sits next to Mr. Gray, pets him awake.

Come on Gary 2, home stretch now. I can almost feel the tears brimming in my eyes. Almost.

Mr. Gray stretches, presents his quivering belly.

I believe in you, Gary 2.

I believe in us.

"WHAT WOULD YOU DO IF I LET YOU GO?" I ASK GARY 2.

He is not speaking to me, has the blanket pulled over his head. I flip the switch on the remote.

"Fuck!" Gary 2 screams, thrashing free of the blanket. "Would you kill me?"

There is something darker than hate in his eyes. In the silence I think I can hear the squeak of his enamel flexing as he clenches his teeth.

"Would you kill me?" I ask, showing him the remote.

"No."

"What would you do?"

He only breathes through his mouth, probably to avoid the stench of the chaos on the floor.

"I would make you suffer. I would cut your mother's eyes out and feed them to you."

I hold up a hand, "She's passed, unfortunately."

Gary 2 is hyperventilating, "I would kill every member of your family in front of you. One by one. But I wouldn't kill you. No. You would suffer. You would beg for me to kill you. I would destroy everything you loved. I would never stop. Never."

I take a breath. Something stirs in that place below my bellybutton.

"Promise?"

"Yes," he spits.

The collar unclasps and falls free of his neck. I place the remote on the nightstand and hop onto the neighboring bed. I fasten the collar around my own neck and secure the lock. (I practiced this all day. When the time came I didn't want to look foolish)

"My address book is on the kitchen counter," I say.

Gary 2 stands, grabs the remote and holds it to his chest. He slinks away, never turning his back to me.

I am incomplete, Mom. I know that now. I also know watching people suffer won't change it.

I hope Gary 2 keeps his word. It's the only way I'll learn.

FROM THE RED DIRT

East of Dumas, Texas – 1933

I buried Grampa as the sun went down, only, he didn't stay that way. Dirt so hard it nearly cracked the shovel. Haven't seen a storm cloud in months, kind of forget the way the land smells after a rain. I just remember I used to like it.

Took most of the afternoon to make the grave deep enough the coyotes couldn't get to him. They're starvin' out here like the rest of us so I can't say I blame 'em. Daddy gave up buryin' the livestock. Wasn't much to bury anyway and the coyotes were mad with hunger. Had to put bullets in 'em and we don't have many of those left.

But it was different with Grampa.

Daddy left day before yesterday. Walked to town to buy a car so we can join up with the folks headed west. It was all the money we had. Everythin'. A life's work fit inside a coffee can, with room to spare. Maybe Grampa was waitin' for him to leave and died on purpose in his rockin' chair so his son wouldn't have to find him that way. Can't say it's much better his grandson found him.

I might've thought he was asleep or in a deep thought. The chair was rockin' with the wind just so, almost looked like he was pushing himself with the toe of his boot. It was the fly that caught my eye. I saw it crawlin' over the creases in his cheek, went straight into his mouth and he didn't flinch from it. I dropped the hammer I was carryin' and grabbed Grampa by the shoulders, shook him, prolly too hard, and his head snapped back like a broken dandelion.

Mama cried and told me to cover him up before my little sister saw. Said I could take him to the barn since there wasn't animals in there, and Daddy would handle it when he got back. But the flies didn't wait for Daddy. Mama went inside and called Jessie upstairs while I stripped the sheets from Grampa's bed. They was yellow and stank of sweat and tobacco, of whiskey spilled from a slumberin' hand. It was his smell, for better or worse, and whatever had been brewin' in his body he didn't tell us about. He bruised easy, took a long time to sit or stand. But Grampa always said the Lord would tell him when his work was done. And so he kept workin' even when there wasn't nothin' to work. You can't make nothin' useful of dirt without rain. All you can do is move it from one place to another.

The wind tipped him halfway out of the rockin' chair when I came back to the porch. His mouth was open and there was a whole mess of flies there, dippin' in and out, goin' in dry and comin' out wet. I laid out the sheet and pulled him onto it. No way to be gentle about it and it upset the flies quite a bit. Sounded like a hornet's nest in his chest.

The worst of it was his eyes opened part way. Though I could only see the bottom half it still felt like he was lookin' at me. Wonder what he would have thought if he *could* see me, eleven years old with tears in my eyes, Mama singin' a hymn to my sister in the background. I wrapped him the best I could, tied a knot in three places so I didn't have to see any part of him.

Grampa wasn't a large man, not that it was possible given our lack of food. But, he was still too heavy for me to carry, so I had to pull him. I grabbed him around the ankles and dragged him over the porch floorboards. Then, I stood for a time, breathin' hard, thinkin' about how I could get him down four stairs without damagin' him too much. Figured it would be less violent to grab him under his arms, but I couldn't stand the thought of his head restin' against my thigh, even with layers of fabric between us.

His skull thudded off each step, a sound I am afraid I will not be able to forget. There wasn't a cloud to block the sun, but off in the distance, in the direction of town, there was a wall of dust the color of old blood. Already, the wind was pickin' up, shootin' little needles of dirt at my neck and face. I pulled Grampa's body over the brittle grass, which crunched under my boots. The wind snaked inside the wrap, fillin' it like a ship's sail. I caught sight of him again, his mouth open with a swarm of flies sippin' whatever moisture was left on his tongue and lips.

The sound of Mama's hymn was eaten by the wind, which had consumed so much of our lives already. I shuffled faster, trippin' over my own boots a few times tryin' to beat the dust cloud. I'd been caught outside in a dust storm before and it gets inside your eyes, ears, in your teeth. Worse, I think some of it got into my spirit. It was like the hopelessness abraded my soul. It killed everythin' we owned, and it was inside of me always.

I made it into the barn with Grampa's body right as the dust hit. Run back to the house as the world went dark. Mama was asleep with Jessie, both of them snorin' right through the storm. It was just me then, sittin' in the dark with my thoughts, listenin' to the wind tear apart our family's livelihood. Kind of sounded like the ocean from a distance, though I'd only been to the coast once in my life and was probably too young to remember it.

A FEW HOURS LATER THE SHEET, ONCE WHITE THEN YELLOW from Grampa's sweat, was a whole different color. Black. It was black with flies desperate to find a respite from the dust and wind. The hollow over his open mouth rippled from the inside, and I knew I could not wait for Daddy. It was an ugly sight, and would get worse overnight, when there was more stirrin' than just flies. I found a spot under the dead oak tree with the low branches I used to play on, and started diggin'. Didn't ask permission, just knew it had to be done. We could speak the words and make a marker for him after he was in the ground.

Mama saw me through the kitchen window, came out with a glass of water. She looked at the hole, about a foot deep then, and cried a bit.

"It's bad, Mama. Just keep Jessie inside."

The sun felt like a coal held just above my neck. The skin of my hands broke, old blisters torn open, but I heard the coyotes in the tall grass. They caught the scent of Grampa's death. I wasn't afraid of even half a dozen mangy coyotes, just one rabid one. So, I kept diggin'.

I pulled Grampa and his new cloak of flies out of the barn and dragged him back over the broken earth. The flies sought the leakin' blisters on my hands and I wanted to scream but didn't have the strength. The sun was settin' then, the coyotes in a frenzy in the field. We didn't have a dog left to chase 'em off. The last dog, Buster, ran away, Daddy said, but there was also meat in the stew that night for the first time in months.

I rolled Grampa into the grave, couldn't bring myself to arrange his body in any specific way, just started shovelin' dirt. I did see an arm was loose of the wrap, a liver-spotted hand quickly covered with the red dirt that defined so much of his life. When it was done and my body felt like it had been trampled to just before dyin', I ripped a few big stones from the ground and placed them atop Grampa's grave. Maybe, I thought, it would keep the coyotes busy.

I slept on the floor beside the fireplace. The stairs might has well have been a mountain. I fell asleep with coyote songs in my ears.

Don't remember dreamin', prolly too tired.

I just remember the sound of Grampa's rockin' chair when I woke, thinkin' it must've been the wind again. Only, it wasn't.

JESSIE SCREAMED, AND THAT WOKE ME UP THE REST OF THE way. I ran with pins and needles in my toes to the porch. She was already gone. I heard her footsteps goin' up the stairs while Mama asked her what was wrong.

There he was, back in his chair. He wore the same overalls, the same boots as the day before. Everythin' was caked in red dirt, like it was his second skin. His head was downcast so I couldn't see his eyes.

"G-G-Grampa?" I said, halfway out the door and thinkin' about goin' back in for Daddy's rifle.

The chair moved a bit, and this time it wasn't the wind. When he lifted his head, I had to hold my hand over my mouth to keep from screamin', felt the floor beneath my feet shift like sand. His mouth opened to speak, but only flies came out, a cloud of 'em like the puff of smoke from a train. After the flies came the soil, mostly dry and clotted, the red dirt I buried him in. My heart felt like it didn't know if it wanted to beat fast or slow, like it could go either way.

"Grampa?"

He looked at me with those dead eyes, flies expelled from his stomach clusterin' there to lap at the moisture.

"Got…to…get ready," he said with a voice like two cornhusks rubbin' together.

He got up from his seat then and retraced the boot prints he left on the porch. There was a cigarette in his right hand, unlit, the kind he rolled himself. It was stained with the same red dirt as the rest of him. My stomach twisted when I noticed the denim around his rear was wet and the greatest number of flies was congregatin' there. He descended the stairs like a baby learnin' its first steps, wobbly at the knees.

I didn't have a thought left. I just watched him walk away, in the direction of the barn. With our livestock dead or sold there wasn't any work left to do, just shorin' up the house against the dust, 'til we could leave all of it behind. But that was where he headed. Think he even whistled, or tried to. Prolly couldn't because of the flies.

"What happened?" Mama asked, eyes like a barn owl.

She pinched her robe closed, worry lines carved deep into her face.

"Grampa came back."

"What?"

"He was dead. You saw it. He was dead. Had flies in his eyes and in his mouth. I-I buried him, put stones over the soil. And he's back."

"No. No. That can't be."

"It is."

We both watched as he opened the barn door and disappeared within, door closin' part way behind him.

"He came back?"

I turned to her and noticed how the shadows scarred her face. She was holdin' on by a thread. For two years she watched the farm collapse into piles of red dirt, watched her husband bend in half from the pressure of keepin' the family together. She smiled when there wasn't cause for it, reassured me and Jessie when there was no real hope, just the memory of it. But, even the strongest steel will bend under enough pressure.

"It's like the stories at church, Mama," I said.

"Church?"

"How Jesus died and came back. Remember?"

She looked off into the distance, prolly recallin' Sunday School lessons from her childhood. I didn't believe in the stories, myself, especially because of all the sufferin' God let happen to us and everyone else in the county. But it was enough for Mama, in that moment, to push her back from the brink of whatever madness she was about to dive into.

"Yes, like Jesus. I remember."

She nodded and smiled, her eyes cloudy like they was lookin' at somethin' I couldn't see.

"Take care of Jessie, okay?" I said.

She ducked back inside the house and within a few moments I heard the sound of pans clatterin'. Don't know what she could be doin' with 'em as we ain't had nothin' to cook in a pan in a long time, just beans in the pot when we can get 'em.

Used to be dew on the grass in the mornin'. Not anymore. It's just as stiff as in the daytime after it's been cookin' under the sun. I followed the broken grass and remnants of Grampa's boot prints. What could he be doin' in the barn? There wasn't a hog to slaughter, no horse hooves to grind. All of it was gone, just the smells left behind.

There wasn't a quiet way to approach. The grass cracked and popped under my weight, like static on the radio before Daddy sold it. I grabbed the handle to slide the barn door open, barely an hour past sunrise and it burned like a hot kettle from the sun. I pulled a bit of my shirt loose of my overalls and wrapped it around my hand, still felt the heat through it.

He was standin' ten feet in front of me, facin' the other way, which was good. There was a sound of metal clankin' together as he rifled through the box of tools.

"Grampa? What are you doin'?"

It was the last question I wanted answered, but I couldn't think of a better one. *How are you standing there? Aren't you dead?* Those were closer to the mark, but no one teaches an eleven year old boy how to talk to a dead man.

"Gotta...get...ready."

"Get ready for what?"

The question hung in the air between us. Maybe it couldn't penetrate the soil still cloggin' his ears. In the absence of his speakin' there was just the sound of flies. Again, they grouped around the wet places. I'd seen plenty of dead things in my life. A calf that wandered too far from its mama and too close to a coyote that was hidin' in the grass. Doesn't take long for carrion to rot in the Texas heat. When it does, all those juices gotta go somewhere. I swallowed but my tongue was dry as leather, thought about what might be goin' on inside Grampa's body.

More metal clangin' and I turned away, closed the barn door leavin' him mostly in darkness. I didn't know what to do, not that a boy my age would have any idea. The Youngs family lived down the road two miles or so, if they hadn't left for California since the last time we spoke. They had only crops, no livestock, so when the rain stopped and the dust took its place they had nothin' to sell. We shared what little we had, but it wasn't enough for a family to live on. Still, Mr. Youngs was a man and he would know better than me what to do.

The air outside the house smelled of somethin' cookin' and my stomach, which was pretty good at stayin' quiet, started rumblin'. I dashed up the steps, forgettin' Grampa for the moment.

Jessie sat at the table, all big-eyed with a fork in one hand and a knife in the other. There was a sizzlin' sound at the stove, where Mama tended to a skillet with her wooden spoon.

"What is it?" I asked.

"Mama's makin' breakfast!" Jessie said, nearly shoutin'.

Mama turned to me, her mouth and eyes tellin' two different stories.

"It's not much, hon, just some potatoes and a bit of dried meat. Your daddy said to save it for a special day. I, uh, don't know if that applies to today, but I didn't know what else to do."

"It smells great, Mama."

I took a seat beside Jessie and mussed her hair. At six years old, she didn't know a life on the farm that wasn't just sufferin'. She didn't know the dusty fields were once green, that the hay in the barn once had a purpose other than just for playin' on.

"How-how is he?" Mama said.

Jessie spoke before I could answer, "Grampa's all dirty! Why'd Grampa get himself so dirty?"

"It's just a game, Jess."

"Can I play?"

I shook my head, "I don't think so. I think the game's over, but we can play another."

"Is he…" Mama began.

"I don't know, Mama. I think he needs to be where he come from. Gotta smell about him, and the flies."

Mama nodded, "Not like Jesus then?"

She turned, skillet in hand, smilin' only with her mouth.

"I don't know, Mama."

She scraped potatoes onto my plate. It was the most food I'd seen since Thanksgiving fellowship at church. When Daddy didn't have enough to tithe we stopped goin', then most everyone left anyway. I forgot about the world while I ate, the salt burnin' my broken lips, but I'd take the pain over hunger any day. Mama had a small plate and took her time eatin', movin' the potatoes around, cuttin' 'em into smaller and smaller pieces to make 'em last. When I heard the creak of the porch steps I shot up from the chair.

"Upstairs, Jessie," I said.

Before she could get mad or ask why Mama nodded and led her that way.

"Tell him I love him and I'm sorry. I just can't see him," Mama said over her shoulder.

The doorknob jiggled. I opened it and backed away. Grampa stumbled inside, boots scrapin' over the floorboards. He smelled awful, like the little pond on the property after it dried up and all the fish died. The flies covered his face like a shiftin' beard. He opened his mouth, maybe to speak, but just coughed, sprayin' flies out.

His eyes looked like old milk when it gets that yellow skin on it. They were furry with flies, stuck open 'cause he couldn't blink. He held a wrench in his right hand, the big one Daddy used on the tractor. We didn't have nothin' he could use it on. I wondered if he was just retracin' his steps from life.

Grampa sat at the table, which took some effort. He sniffed Mama's potatoes, but it rattled in his throat when he did. His face and neck was swollen in places, the wrinkled skin stretched taught. There was liquid runnin' out of his ear like rust water. Tears stung my eyes and I turned away. He was like my second daddy. When Daddy was over my left shoulder teachin' me how to do somethin' Grampa was over the right sayin' not to listen to him.

"Grampa, why'd you come back?"

I accepted he was dead. His body was breakin' down in front of me. But I also accepted he was sittin' at the table smellin' Mama's potatoes like he did in life. He didn't look about to speak, so I left him there. Hadn't changed my shirt in days and my neck was grimy from sweat. Figured a wash rag and a new shirt might help me think. Daddy said he wouldn't come back without a car. I knew how much was in the coffee can. It wasn't enough. Maybe someone would take pity on him.

WHEN THE KNOCK CAME I THOUGHT IT WAS GRAMPA. I'D heard the chair scrape over the floorboards and the front door open a half hour before. Thought maybe he forgot how to get back inside. The girls were in the kitchen cleanin' the mess from breakfast, and so I ran to answer the knock before Jessie could.

He had backed off the porch, was standin' in the yard in front of the steps.

"Help you, mister?" I said.

He was a weathered man with a scar across his nose, like it was cut off and stitched back together. By his feet was a sack with the handle of a pot stickin' out. His clothes hung on him like he stole 'em from someone half a foot taller. The boots were mismatched and of different sizes. His cap was like the ones kids sellin' newspapers in big cities wore, and it prolly didn't do much to block the sun.

"Man of the house around?" he said.

He looked past me at the front door as Mama peeked through it, Jessie wormin' her way under her arm so she could see.

"In the field. What can I do for you?" I said.

The man glanced to the right and then behind. There wasn't nothin' livin' out that way and his smirk showed that he knew it.

"Just lookin' for work is all. If he's not here…"

There was a railroad a few miles east. On quiet nights I could hear trains thunderin' down the tracks. Sometimes it slowed if there was cattle passin' through. If it slowed enough some of the tramps that ride the rails would hop off there. It wasn't the first time one came by askin' for work. It was how he didn't look at me, how he pinned his black overcoat to his body with one hand, like he was afraid of the wind catchin' it and me seein' somethin' I wasn't supposed to. It was the fact he danced around without speakin' it. Daddy was gone. There was no man of the house.

"Like I said, he's out in the field. Had to put an old bull down. Broke its leg."

The man looked down so I would not see him smile.

"Happy to work for supper. If he's plannin' on butcherin' it."

I gritted my teeth, "I'll be sure to tell him."

The man nodded and tipped his cap at Mama.

"Ma'am. Little lady," he said and then turned away, walkin' slow like he was underwater.

I only noticed when he disappeared from my line of sight my fingernails were carvin' sickle shapes in my palms.

"Is it okay, Joseph?" Mama asked.

I shook my head no.

"Left too quick I think. If a starvin' man gives up easy it's cause he's got another plan brewin'. Can you get Daddy's rifle?"

She stepped out of the house and stood beside me, lookin' at the place he disappeared.

"He took it with him."

"What?"

Mama put an arm around my shoulder and my back stiffened some. It wasn't a good feelin', not like it had been before.

"He had all of our money, son. All of it. Couldn't risk losin' it."

There was little strength left in her fingers. She squeezed, tryin' to reassure, but it just reminded me of how broken she was.

"It'll be okay, Mama."

When I lie, I try to do it over important things. Our house, the paint chipped away by blowin' dust, was a gray island in a sea of brown. My first thought was to gather the girls and make a run for the Youngs property. But I had a feelin' the man hadn't gone far, was maybe waitin' just beyond the little rise in the land that met up with the dirt road. Figured it'd be better on a gray island than in a sea when I couldn't see what was in the water.

I SAW GRAMPA BY THE DEAD OAK TREE. THOUGHT HE MIGHT jump back in the hole he climbed out of, but he only looked at it. The denim of his overalls was dark, and the right arm was swollen some, bulgin' against the seams of his shirt. I wanted to yell at him to just get in the hole. Had enough to worry about without my dead Grampa stumblin' around the property, body balloonin' up in the heat.

I spent the whole afternoon lookin' for weapons in case the tramp came back. I would've traded everythin' in that damn coffee can to have Daddy here, with or without his rifle. The house still smelled of breakfast, but there wasn't anythin' quite so good for supper. One potato split three ways with a bit of broth spiced with the burnt bits of meat she scraped off the skillet. I had the mallet Daddy used to put down cows, but it was too heavy for me to swing. Maybe just the sight of it would be enough.

Jessie chatted while we ate, tellin' us what she thought California might be like. A family from church went that way a few months back and the daughter, who was a year older than Jessie, sent a letter talkin' about strawberries the size of a baby's fist. By the end of the meal, I was hungrier than when it started. But I would never get in the way of Jessie dreamin' out loud. It's just tellin' yourself stories, which we all needed then.

Mama sent Jessie up to get ready for bed. It was still light, but the shadows were stretched out and I could hear coyotes, likely gettin' stirred up from Grampa's death smell.

"What're you gonna do with that, Joseph?" Mama asked, nodding at the mallet.

"Hopefully nothin'. If need be I'll do like Daddy showed me."

"It's not right. You're just a boy."

"There's no right or wrong about it, Mama. I don't need to kill him. I just need to keep him from gettin' to Jessie. If he makes it past me that'll be your job."

Mama nodded. She rummaged through a drawer next to the sink and pulled out a knife then dropped it in the pocket of her apron.

"Leave the window open in case you need to jump," I said.

We hugged for a long time. I felt the warmth of her tears soak into my shirt, though I didn't hear her cry.

"It'll be okay, Mama. Maybe Daddy will come drivin' up in a car tonight."

It wasn't a lie. Just tellin' myself a story.

"Maybe so," Mama said.

I PULLED A CHAIR UP TO THE WINDOW IN THE SITTIN' ROOM. I cracked it a bit and listened to the sounds of the day givin' way to night. Figured I would hear him before I saw him, the grass crunchin' under his mismatched boots. It was so dark at night, even with a half moon and no clouds. From where I sat all I could see was shadows, and all of 'em looked like the tramp with the stupid hat.

An hour after dark I had to pinch myself to keep from noddin' off. I got up from the chair and walked around the room, checked the lock on the door at the back of the house. I suppose if I was the tramp I would likely use that door instead of the one I guarded. I'd wedged a chair under the doorknob, but it wouldn't survive a couple of good kicks.

I imagined how it would go down between the tramp and me. I'd hold the mallet with one hand up near the head of it and the other grippin' the handle. If I could jab it at his stomach I could stun him, knock the air out of his lungs. After that I didn't know. Couldn't do much else with the mallet that wouldn't haunt me for the rest of my life.

I snapped my eyes open, only then realizin' I'd drifted into a dream. My chin rested on my forearms and a bit of drool was leakin' out the side of my mouth. Why was I awake? Some sound I heard on the edge of the dream, but it planted itself in that part of my mind, and I couldn't recall it.

My eyes adjusted to the dark some, enough so I could tell the shapes apart. I put my ear next to the openin' and listened for the sound to come again. It did after a few seconds, voices. Not *one* voice. Voices.

I stood up, mallet in hand. Felt impossible to wield, like I was a kid playin' knight with a man's sword.

"Your daddy cut up that bull?" the tramp said, not hidin' anymore.

I didn't know what to say. Maybe I could make my voice deeper, but I don't think it would fool him.

He laughed, "I didn't think so. I think your daddy is dead or gone away. That makes you the man of the house now. Isn't that right?"

I opened my mouth but didn't have any words ready.

"Oh, come on. I can see you in there. Holdin' somethin' it looks like."

I gripped the mallet tighter.

"Hope it's bulletproof."

Some of the strength bled out of my legs.

"Now I know you ain't got much. Barely got four walls and a roof. Wouldn't be worth it to rob you. What if I just take shelter for the night? Think your mama would mind the company?"

"Go to hell!" I yelled.

"Ha ha! There he is!"

There was a sound of the doorknob rattlin' behind me.

"Sorry, brought a friend with me. Hope that's okay. That's Long Jake back there. Don't know how he got the nickname. He ain't exactly tall. Gotta nasty case of syphilis, though. Maybe *Long* is referrin' to somethin' else," the tramp said, laughing again.

The door shuddered from an impact.

"And if *I'm* keepin' your mama company, I guess Long Jake will have to make do with the little lady."

The door shuddered again.

"Well, that's rude of me, isn't it? I can see you but you can't see me? You know, it's awful dark in there. Care for a little light?"

There was a brief spark and then the flame grew. He stood off to the side of the porch steps some, holdin' a bottle up near his face, burnin' rag hangin' out of it.

"Think I could make it through that open window up there?"

He held the bottle back like he was gonna throw it.

"No!" I yelled.

I ran to the front door and grabbed the knob, not really thinkin' about it. I unlocked it, but didn't open it. It was what he wanted. He wanted me to come out. The back door rattled again, wood sounded like it was splinterin' some. I couldn't fight 'em both off, maybe not at all and definitely not runnin' from one to the other.

"Fire's gettin' hot over here, young man," the tramp said.

The door behind shook, chair bucklin'. Then it went quiet for a moment. Felt like a long time but probably wasn't. Then a scream. Thought Long Jake might be gettin' ready to bust through, but it wasn't that kind of scream. I backed away from the front door and took a couple steps toward the other man. Another scream and I started runnin'.

The tramps was fightin' behind the house. No idea why, but it was the best I could hope for. I kicked aside the broken chair and pressed my nose to the window. It wasn't the tramp. I opened the door and stepped outside. My eyes adjusted some, not enough to see color, but one man was on the ground with his hand up, the other standin' over him.

"Grampa?" I said.

"N-n-no!" the other man yelled, scootin' backwards.

The smell hit me then and it felt like my stomach flipped upside down. I covered my mouth, but the smell changed the taste on my tongue to somethin' rotten. Grampa lifted the wrench with his left hand. In life he was right-handed, but the right arm was swole like it was about to pop. He brought the wrench down, not fast but it was heavy. The man on the ground seemed injured already, and he hid behind his arm instead of deflectin' the blow. The wrench caught him in the teeth, and the next scream was choked with blood.

I just stood there, not knowin' what to do. Long Jake coughed blood and prolly any teeth he had left. He was lookin' at the blood spillin' on his chest and not at the wrench Grampa held above his head.

Two quick explosions. The wrench fell out of Grampa's hand. The tramp with the stupid hat was standin' about ten feet away. Didn't bring the fire with him.

"Grampa!"

I ran a few steps toward him, but the odor drove me back. Grampa looked at his belly, touched it with his fingers. The smell of gun smoke mixed with the stench of rot. I dropped to my knees and vomited my supper.

Click

Click

The tramp flipped his gun around so that the grip was facin' out. He walked toward Grampa and I realized I couldn't lift the mallet. My hands felt like they wasn't mine anymore, like I couldn't control 'em. I was about to watch Grampa die for a second time.

"Guess you wasn't lyin' about your daddy. What the fuck is wrong with him? Smells worse than pig shit."

The tramp reared back at the same time Grampa turned to face him. I couldn't see Grampa well in the dark, just the shape of him, but the tramp saw him just fine.

"W-what? W-what the fuck?"

He took a step back as Grampa came toward him. The tramp tripped, stumblin' backwards, gun slippin' from his fingers. Grampa stood over him. He touched his belly, probed the exit wound with his finger.

"What the fuck?" the tramp said, boots comin' free as he scooted.

Grampa's hand came loose of his stomach with a wet, suckin' sound. Looked like he had a mound of mashed potatoes in his hand, but they was black and the smell got worse real quick. Grampa collapsed onto the tramp, who wouldn't stop screamin'. He beat Grampa in the head with open palms, but I doubt Grampa could feel it. Long Jake was sittin' upright, touchin' the ruins of his mouth.

The tramp found his gun and prolly was about to use it. He opened his mouth to scream, but it ended quick, as Grampa shoved the handful of whatever he pulled out of his stomach into the tramp's mouth. Grampa pinched the tramp's nostrils and hovered just over him. The tramp gurgled and thrashed suckin' the rotten entrails into his lungs. Grampa's face was just a couple inches from the tramp's. Then they was connected by a black stream of clotted flies and filth, as more of what was rotten in his belly was expelled, fillin' the tramp's mouth.

Long Jake was standin'. He looked at the wrench and then at Grampa. Couldn't see his eyes in the dark. Couldn't guess what he was thinkin', jaw hangin' onto the skull by sinew, his buddy chokin' to death just a few feet from him. He didn't look at me. He didn't look at the house. He walked into the tall, dry grass, trailin' blood.

The tramp's arm was movin' but his legs was still. He wasn't fightin' anymore, just wavin' his hand like shooin' a fly. Plenty of those around him. That stopped after a few seconds, and then it was quiet again. Three souls and I was the only one breathin'.

Coyote yaps came soon after from the tall, dry grass. A couple more screams, not a whole lot behind 'em.

"Grampa?" I said.

I couldn't bring myself to touch him, to come any closer. I could still smell him.

I didn't even thank him as he stood, the river of gore between his mouth and the dead tramp's snappin'. He walked forward, into the night, in the direction of the dead oak tree. To the red dirt that defined so much of his life.

I called to him again, but he didn't turn back. His head was angled at the sky listenin' to somethin' I couldn't hear, the Lord I imagine, tellin' him his work was done.

No coyote songs that night. They was too busy eatin'. When I woke the next mornin' there wasn't a whole lot left to bury.

MAMA AND ME DIDN'T TELL DADDY THE TRUTH OF WHAT happened, not the whole truth. Even the part about the tramps nearly broke him, and there's only so many times you can break a man before he can't right himself. Grampa was a hero. Took down two thugs with just a wrench, sacrificin' himself in the process. Daddy didn't need to know the other part, about how Grampa came back. It made it harder to leave, though, knowin' Grampa was in the dirt we put in the rearview mirror of Daddy's Ford. I just hoped he'd stay there.

UNDER NO CIRCUMSTANCES

Hector jogged to catch up to the old caretaker who, despite his age, understood the cemetery terrain and knew which tufts of grass would buckle into ankle-snapping sinkholes. Abe dodged hidden tree roots without breaking stride as Hector lined through haphazard text in his pocket notebook, days and times the lawn was mowed. He could not read a word he'd written, stumbling as he had, and so whispered the schedule to imprint it in his memory.

"Don't need to worry too much about the mowin'. It doesn't have anythin' to do with your job, son. Just wanted you to know 'cause the mowed grass can do a number on your shoes. I suggest *black* shoes if you don't have a pair already," the old man said.

Abe stopped, hands perched on hips, and surveyed the sprawling cemetery as if seeing it for the first time. He carried himself with a nobility few men who wore their name as a patch over their left breast pocket could muster. Hector used the brief respite to jot a few notes. The job paid well, likely due to the hours and location, but he wasn't sure what the duties were. For the past hour, he'd followed Abe around the tombstones learning the history of both the cemetery and the town.

"Whisper is one of those places that shouldn't exist, right? Everybody was movin' west toward California back then, but along the way some people just gave up, planted their flag in this great big empty. Trains connected the towns that survived. The others dried up and the wind did the rest. Cowards is what they were. Acted like the land was free for the takin'. Like there wasn't already people here."

Abe spat on the ground, hands like sledgehammers at his sides.

"There *was* people, just not the kind that stayed in one place long. There was a whole history here, passed down in stories and songs," Abe said, smiling, eyes scanning the horizon. "And there was more. But those cowards wouldn't understand."

Hector read his notes, "So, the grass is cut every Tuesday during the spring, and every other Wednesday during the summer?"

Abe nodded, turned and angled for the shade of an oak tree.

"Back here the grass is allowed to grow a bit wild. This is the original cemetery from the mid-1800s. Can't read the names on the stones anymore. Suffice it to say, won't nobody complain 'bout the state of their great auntie's plot. Nobody's *alive* that remembers 'em."

The old man sneered. He gave one of the tombstones a little kick with the toe of his boot as he passed it.

Hector stepped carefully through the tall grass, testing the ground in front of him before trusting it.

"Mr. Abraham…"

"Abe."

"Abe, I appreciate all of the information, but I wasn't hired as lawn maintenance. I don't think I was, I mean. I can help if you need it. I'm not above lawn work. I guess I just don't know what I actually signed up for."

Abe paused and glanced at his watch. He looked to the west as if to verify the sun was in the proper place.

"How about we have a quick bite? Should be the right time to tell you about the job after," Abe said.

"Okay."

Abe kicked another of the old tombstones as he passed. Hector did the same.

"Sorry I don't have much to offer. Just the shakes for me. It's what keeps me goin'," Abe said, lifting his Thermos in a *cheers* motion.

"That's okay. I ate before I came," Hector said. The bread of the peanut butter and jelly sandwich Abe provided was so brittle it might as well have been a cracker.

The caretaker's cottage was cozy but mostly barren. The kitchen appeared to have never fulfilled its purpose previously. There were no pots on the stove, no cups drying on a dish towel. The ancient refrigerator bled rust along its seams and rattled continuously as Abe spoke.

"So, you *live* in the cemetery?" Hector asked.

Abe nodded and wiped his lips, quickly checking his sleeve before replying, "Yeah, it works out. Don't spend much time in here, but it's nice to have a place to rest my feet."

Abe arched his eyebrows at the ink spilling out of the sleeves of Hector's work shirt, "Nice tats. Where'd you get 'em?"

Hector scratched back of his neck, hot like a tomato on the vine after a day in the Texas sun.

"Um, most were *inside*."

Abe waited for Hector to finish.

"I was locked up for a while, as you know. Nothing violent. I mean, I appreciate the opportunity you're giving me here. I, uh, still don't know exactly what the work entails."

"Well, who am I to judge a man for somethin' he did to survive, whether it was necessary or not? Folk do all kinds of things to survive."

"I'm grateful. I applied all over town for the past two months. Was running out of options that wouldn't put me behind bars again, until you called me back."

Abe downed the rest of his shake and patted his belly, "That goes down smooth. Don't know if I'll ever get used to takin' my meals outta bottle, but we make do, don't we?"

Hector forced a chuckle, "Yes. Yes, we do."

Abe stood at the sink, Thermos hovering under the faucet. He turned, "You know, it takes a special kind of person to do this job. Not just because of the hours, although there's not a lotta people pinin' for the midnight shift in a cemetery. It's lonely work, but I imagine you know a deal about that."

Hector nodded, "I do."

"No wife and kids? No one at home?"

Hector shook his head, "No one stuck around."

Abe checked his watch, turned and peered at the gauzy shadows creeping across the lawn.

"I guess we can finish our tour, huh? You're probably gonna have a lot of questions at the end of it. Some I can't answer. This isn't a job with a future, son. I suppose when you get your life on track you'll be onto better things. But the position opened unexpectedly. Mr. Ralph had been with us for some time. Was good at his job, but it can wear you down. Guess it wore him down enough."

COOL, GRAY FINGERS OF MIST COILED AROUND TREE TRUNKS. Crickets chirped on dewy blades of grass as the night leeched the sun-baked warmth from the tombstones. Hector once again struggled to keep up with Abe, who navigated without thinking about it while continuing his town and cemetery education.

"First folks in Whisper weren't the first folks, obviously. Texas had only been a state for a decade at that time. Them *settlers* was just the first folks who could put ink to paper to say they were there. The tribes passed through this land for thousands of years before a wagon wheel ever touched this earth. They had no paper, just those stories and songs passed from one generation to the next. Don't make 'em any less true. I liked the ones about their gods the best."

Abe stroked his silver, silken braids and waited for Hector to catch up.

"That's really interesting Mr. Abe. I hope this doesn't sound rude, but does it have anything to do with my job?"

Abe stepped forward and clamped a hand on Hector's shoulder.

"Just givin' a bit of context. Can't tell you everythin' at once or you'll think I'm off my rocker."

Hector reflexively recoiled from the old man's breath. He could not imagine drinking something that would make breath smell like that. A mixture of chalk and rubber, like the vitamins his grandma took for her heart.

"What do you mean?"

Abe directed Hector's gaze to a mausoleum in the distance.

"That's where we're headed. That's your job."

Hector frowned and shook his head.

"If you listen to every word I say…if you follow my instructions, you can have a job here for as long as you like. Like I said, you'll probably move onto better things, but we're happy to have you for now. Ralph was a good employee, but he stopped following instructions."

"What happened? Did you fire him?" Hector asked, swallowing the knot in his throat.

Abe aimed his finger at some point in the distance, hidden by a thickening fog.

"That's his plot over there. He'll be buried on Friday. What's left of him."

"What's left…"

Abe patted Hector on the back and headed toward the mausoleum. Over his shoulder he said, "They're real easy instructions to follow. Don't worry about that. You can fit every word on one page of your little notebook and have half a page to spare."

Hector withdrew the notebook, "My job is the…" he trailed off, forgetting the proper term for the large, cube structure.

"The mausoleum, yes. That's your job."

Hector rubbed his hands together. It felt twenty degrees cooler than when he arrived.

"Cleaning it?"

Abe shook his head, "Not quite."

Hector returned the notebook to his pocket, looked in the direction of the parking lot. His car was somewhere in that fog. Though he was still grateful, he was approaching the end of his patience, and that was something he had in abundance after prison.

The mausoleum looked as old as the oldest tombstones in the cemetery. There was no towering obelisk, no Corinthian columns or decaying busts. It was set back from the tombstones, shadowed under the branches of an oak twitching in the light breeze. The iron bars surrounding it extended to its roof.

"Looks like one of those jails from the Westerns," Hector said, then nodded at the iron bars. "What's in there they're afraid of someone stealing?"

Abe smiled, teeth like a mouthful of fireflies, "Not tryin' to keep people out," he said, then scratched his head. "Well, I suppose that's part of it."

There was a folding chair in front of the mausoleum, facing the door. Abe pointed at it, "That's for you. Feel free to dress it up if you want. Ralph had a little cushion but it, uh, well the stains wouldn't come out."

Hector stood beside the chair but did not sit.

"This is my job? To sit in front of this…thing?"

Abe nodded, "They named this town Whisper because of the way the wind sounds passin' through the fields. There were other names for it before. Some I have forgotten, sad to say."

He stepped away from the fading shadows of the trees overhead, checked his watch again.

"If I close my eyes, I can remember what it was like. I can hear the wind, just beyond it the sound of drums, of feet tapping the earth. I can hear their voices. That's why I stay, why I didn't move on. It's how I know I didn't just dream it all."

Hector sat, "I don't understand."

Abe dabbed at his eyes, "So much was lost. So many songs never to be sung again, stories never told."

He tapped his head, "But I remember."

"Abe?"

"Your job is simple. Under no circumstances will you unlock that door until the sun fully rises. If it's cloudy and you're not sure if the sun is up, just wait another fifteen minutes. Don't abuse that for overtime. Be honest about it."

Hector began to rise, shaking his head, "Why does it need to be unlocked at all? There's just some dead people in there, right?"

Abe gripped his shoulder, the strength in his fingers making Hector's stomach turn.

"That's a *yes and no* question if I've ever heard one. You are going to hear pleas for mercy, pleas to be let out. You are going to be insulted and harassed, belittled and mocked. Mock right on back if you want to. Just stay engaged. Don't sit there in silence."

"Wh-what is...why?"

"It's like the mean dog behind the fence. It'll bark at folks walkin' by all day, never tirin' of it, never any less angry. Take away its reason for barkin', though, and it'll get to work on other mischief. It'll get to work on findin' a way out."

Hector chewed his lip, searched for the parking lot hidden beneath the fog.

"I don't know if I can."

"Sure you can, son. Just those two things you need to remember and nothin' else. I could tell you more, but it would complicate things, lead to other questions," Abe said, then eyed the rising moon. "And we don't have the time for that now. Some of it you'll figure out. Look, there's just a couple of people on this earth that know about this place. You're one of 'em. The others, well, they ain't gonna say anythin'. I keep my job and they keep quiet."

Abe lifted Hector's hand, peeled open the fingers and dropped a thick skeleton key onto the palm.

"Lock it. And what else?" Abe asked.

"What else?"

"The rules. What are they?"

Hector swallowed, pressed his left hand to his roiling belly.

"Under no circumstances do I unlock the door until the sun rises. Stay engaged."

Abe nodded, "You can take a break if you need. Fifteen or so minutes at the most. Any more than that won't be good for you or anyone else."

"I don't…"

Abe retreated a step, stroked his braids, "Some folk, when meetin' somethin' they don't understand for the first time, they try to learn about it. Most don't. Most go the other way 'cause some old book said their god wouldn't allow such things to exist. Those folks," Abe said, then pivoted and pointed. "Those folks are just piles of bones turnin' to dust. Me? I'm still here."

Abe skipped up the mausoleum steps jackrabbit-quick. With his back to Hector, he unbuttoned his shirt, folded it, and placed it on the concrete. Then, he kicked off his shoes, removed his pants and repeated the exercise.

"Mind gettin' the door?" he asked.

Hector slid off the chair, "Uh, sure."

Abe stepped into the pure dark of the mausoleum. A pair of folded, moon-white briefs emerged and were placed within arm's reach of the heavy door.

"Close it."

Hector did. There was silence for a moment, then Abe spoke again, voice muffled, "Lock it, son."

Hector obeyed, tugged the lock a few times to make sure, then returned to the chair.

"What the fuck is this?" he whispered, rubbing his hands together as he eyed the door. He left the chair, scaled the steps again.

He knocked on an iron bar, as they were grouped too closely together to allow his hand to pass through to reach the door.

"Abe? What is this? What's going on?"

Abe cleared his throat. His voice was small, as if he'd wandered to the opposite end of the room.

"That's a question I can't answer. Remember what I said about questions leadin' to other questions?"

"Yeah, I just…"

"I'm not pretendin' it ain't strange for you. If I was in your shoes I'd be wonderin' just the same. But if I answer that question your bound to have another, pretty soon you're gonna find yourself unlockin' the door 'cause we got all conversational and you forgot the rules."

Hector nodded and tucked the key into his jeans pocket. He sauntered back to the chair and sat, the cool night air like a silk sheet caressing his exposed skin. He withdrew his pen and notebook, but it was too dark to read. The pads of his fingertips traced the impressions the pen carved into the paper. He could make out a few letters just by feel.

His mind drifted to a familiar place, one often visited in moments of solitude. He thought of his first night in the cell. Jail was its own nightmare, but the transient nature of its populace made it feel less *real*. "Lights out" in prison was a different experience entirely. It was quiet to begin, then the whispering started. Hissing.

"Hey…Mustache. Where you from Mustache? Who you with?"

Hector didn't realize his neighbor was speaking to him.

"Hey, fucker. Talkin' to you. Who you with?"

He rubbed his hands together, that cold feeling, as if the iron in his blood turned to ice, spread from his heart to his fingertips. He didn't know the right answer, didn't know what the man in the cell next to him wanted to hear. He wasn't *with* anyone.

"Okay, Hector, time to let me out."

Hector looked up, unsure if it was a memory.

"What?"

The voice was clearer, as if Abe had pressed his lips directly to the door's seam.

"Time to let me out."

"But, you said…the rules."

"Yeah, the rules. They're not for me. They're for what comes next. Let me out and I'll tell you the rest."

Hector glanced over his shoulder, crosses and angel wings protruding through an ocean of fog. There was no supervisor, no boss man to provide direction.

"Abe?"

"Yes, now let me out. I'm *old* you stupid, stupid man. Let me out!"

BAM!

The door thrummed from the impact, iron bars singing in the stillness of the night.

Hector stood, felt the key in his pocket. He whipped his head around searching for the parking lot.

What were the rules? There were only two, right? Did Abe say anything about who they were for?

"What are you waiting for? You want the job?"

Hector cleared his throat, "Y-yes."

"Good. Let me out or your fired."

Hector reached inside his pocket, "I-I can't Mr. Abraham. Y-you said I only-"

"Had two rules. I know. But they're not for me. They sent you to prison as dumb as you are? Isn't there a special place for people like you? Open the fucking door."

BAM! BAM! BAM!

Hector's skin radiated heat. His fingernails carved trenches into his palms.

"I'm not dumb."

"Oh you're not? Don't you know who I am? If you weren't dumb you would have opened the door by now. Mama's gonna be real disappointed in you, Hector. I bet you told her you got the job, didn't you?"

"I didn't…"

"Now you're gonna have to tell her you didn't last one hour of the first night. Doesn't that sound like something a fucking moron would do? Lose his job on the first night?"

"I'm not a…"

What did Abe say about engaging? Hector was supposed to give it back, right? But he failed to mention Abe was the person he would be giving it to.

"Not a what? A stupid fucking felon, desperate to keep a midnight job in a cemetery staring at a pile of stones and some iron bars?"

"Mr. Abraham, why are you saying these things? What did I do to-"

Abe laughed, a thunderous sound Hector could not imagine originating in the small, bird-like chest of the cemetery caretaker. The iron bars sang again.

For a moment that stretched into two, the cemetery was still, the faint ringing in Hector's ears fading to nothing. Wind turned the dry leaves of nearby trees into rattles, and a coyote introduced itself to the night.

"Mr. Abraham?"

It didn't feel right to call him Abe.

Silence from the mausoleum.

He could just leave.

But could he leave Abe locked inside the mausoleum? Who else knew of this ritual? Abe said only a couple of people on earth did, and would any of them come looking for him? Hector scratched his head, the hair soft enough to manipulate after having shaved it most of the past decade. Abe made some comparison to a dog, something about how it would turn its attention to escape if it wasn't engaged.

Laughter again, like the echo of a distant mountain crumbling to pebbles.

"You stood right next to me and didn't suspect? You smelled it on my breath, didn't you? Just imagine what I'll do to you. You'll kill your mother to go back to prison."

The voice was not Abe's, not the Abe he knew, brief as their interaction was. It was the voice of something unaccustomed to human speech, as if the throat was only ever intended to scream.

Hector whispered, "Smelled it on your breath?"

The pieces were there, but he had trouble making sense of them.

"W-what are you?" Hector asked.

Abe, or whatever was speaking to him, did not respond. In the absence of his terrible voice, the silence that followed felt as vast as the space between the stars. Minute by minute, nightbirds pierced holes in the quiet. The wind shook dead leaves free from their branches. Hector alternated between sitting on the chair and circling the mausoleum at a respectful distance.

He had no watch, and the cell phone was in the car. Abe told him not to bring those items for at least the first week.

You need to trust your eyes and your intuition.

Hector sat and listened. He waited, palm cupping his chin, watching the ghostly gray stones, the iron bars blurring in and out of focus.

Occasionally, a volley of insults emerged from the tomb, the haggard voice sounding more animal than man. It spoke truths about Hector he never shared with the world. He responded, conviction waning as the hours dragged.

"Convinced yourself you were innocent, did you not? Wrote your mother the same thing from your cell. Innocent of many crimes, but there were many more they could have taken you for."

"Shut up," Henry said, eyes unfocused as he traveled through time. He was just a kid. He didn't know any better.

"Your mind is so full of excuses it is a wonder there is room for any other thoughts. You fool. Look at you. Look where you are. Surrounded by dead people, inches from death yourself."

"You don't know..."

"And somehow, she's still proud of you. Your lies are like a hymn to her, one lulling her to sleep, to dream of a better life and a better son."

Hector nearly fell asleep, himself, the whispering of wind through the trees returning him to the cold comfort of his cell and the endless chatter of four-hundred men attempting to assure themselves they existed. His eyelids were coated with honey. Toward the end of his time, he became one of them, confessing his sins to no one in particular, the faint echo of his own words reflecting off the cell wall assuring him he did exist. But he did not speak them all. Those hidden words were like ichor in his belly.

"It's time."

Hector shot to his feet in a pugilist's stance. He saw the stone building, the iron bars, and for a moment existed in two worlds at once.

"Hector, it's time."

Realization washed over him like the gray light creeping across the dewy cemetery grounds.

"Abe?"

"Yes, you did good, son. The job is yours."

Hector turned to the east. It was cloudy in that direction, the rising sun's light smothered by fog. He couldn't see the sun, could only guess where it was in the sky.

"Abe, I, um, I can't see the sun all the way. You said to wait ten minutes if I wasn't sure, right?"

Abe's voice was hoarse, sounded very much like the old man he presented himself to be.

"Okay, son, just…don't make me wait too long," he said, then added, "Please."

Hector readied the key. He counted in his head but lost track around two hundred, began again and lost track at about the same place. It was brighter, gray light warming to yellow. How many minutes was two hundred plus two hundred?

Hector inserted the key into the lock. At the sound, Abe spoke again, "Remember I said they named the town Whisper because of the sound the wind makes on the plains?"

Hector popped the hasp, bent to retrieve Abe's clothes, "Yes, I remember."

"That's what they say now, but it wasn't the truth back then."

He removed the lock and tilted the stack of clothes so they would fit through the crack.

"It wasn't just the whisper of the wind. It was the whisper in the night. The whisper of something they didn't understand."

Hector slid the clothes through the gap between the door and its frame. His forearm was seized by a slick hand, the fingers like constricting pythons. Hector gasped, strained to break free.

In the darkness of the mausoleum, yellow eyes shone like twin suns hurtling towards a black abyss.

"For them, as it will be for you, the last sound you hear in this life."

URBEX

When the jobs left Michigan the infrastructure stayed behind, monuments to a glimpse of prosperity. Negligence, punctuated by brutal winters, disassembled mankind's best intentions, infecting them with rust and rot, eroding the mortar until it crumbled like beach sand.

It was my playground. Hospitals and mansions, factories and schools. All abandoned and caught between the things they were and the things they would become. Documenting that strange wilderness helped me better understand myself, my mortality. Time and circumstances meant some buildings were shielded from decay while others were not. Just as a person with no family history of cancer might find themselves nodding as a doctor forecasts the success of certain interventions. Tough to dodge a bullet you didn't know was coming. It was a harmless addiction, one that cleared the stale air from my lungs, until it wasn't.

Leave no trace. For new urban explorers, this is the Golden Rule. Take nothing from the site and leave no evidence you were there. Become a ghost, essentially. Easy enough for me. There are other rules. Dozens depending on how far down the Reddit-hole you want to go.

Never travel alone. Always share your location and an expected time of return. A woman, unaccompanied, scouring the ruins of American Progress might as well be gift-wrapped and left on a platter, ass-up if you'll forgive the crude imagery, which I cannot claim as my own. Yes, there are homeless, runaways, and others living on society's periphery. Unaccounted for. Unwatched. In my experience, the folks in hiding don't want to be found, and they've usually fled before my headlamp can spot them.

Fellow explorers, however, are a mixed bag. Territorial. I've never been mountaineering but imagine it would be similar to reaching the summit of a secret peak to find someone standing on it, their flag already planted. Exclusivity drives us to more obscure locales. Off the map. Forgotten.

While honoring the Golden Rule, I relaxed my approach to the others. I was searching for my hidden Everest, and I was determined to find it alone.

I TOLD NO ONE. IT ISN'T A SECRET IF YOU SHARE IT WITH THE world.

I don't know what the building was intended to be, far from a major population center. There were no signs, no loose letters hanging from old nails. At a glance, it was untouched by human hands other than those that built it and later boarded the windows before its purpose could be fulfilled. It was like the first tombstone in a cemetery that never welcomed another.

I found it using Google Earth, scanning vast swaths of green for tiny patches of gray. Not quite a needle in a haystack, but it does tire the eyes. It was northwest of Saginaw, an ovular gap of cleared trees with a gray rectangle at its center. I found no mention of what it was or might have been online. No posts in any forum I frequented. I planned the drive and fully expected some barrier to present itself, but none did. There was no gate, no security. The road was rough but doable for my Jeep.

There she was, a block of bricks erupting from a chest-high meadow. The surrounding forest encroached with tentative advances, saplings with a few winters in their rings. Vines snaked over the façade like little green rivers, searching for cracks in the mortar. The Greek columns were common for small town municipal buildings. I hoped I was wrong about that. Old government sites do not become more fascinating with time.

There was no graffiti. The building's wear was an effect of time and weather, not bored teenagers. It was my mountain, my hidden Everest.

I snapped a few pictures with my cell, easier to post on social media when I felt comfortable revealing the secret, then pocketed it in favor of the Nikon in my backpack. The sun dipped below the pines, taking much of its light. As my eyes adjusted, the structure appeared held together by the ivy, the vines fighting collapse rather than accelerating it.

The surrounding forest responded to the sudden change in temperature. Toads napping beneath sun-warmed leaves offered grating bellows as crickets teased them with songs like squeaky hinges. I could not see my breath but felt the late summer chill in my ears as I took close-ups of the threadlike cracks in the columns.

I thought the cockroach was a blemish, a chunk of stone that flaked free and filled with shadow. Maybe it was a scout.

The benefits of hindsight.

It descended the column, skittering toward me as if I was a patch of darkness on a suddenly illuminated kitchen floor. If I was more afraid of cockroaches, I might have stopped there. Might have interpreted this as an omen. Instead, I simply found a new target to photograph, working my way around the side of the building, as the front door was boarded shut.

There is beauty in decay. Or maybe that's just something I tell myself. My eyes seek the imperfections, the chipped concrete holding a story it will never share.

My family and friends were not inspired by the decay spreading inside my body. They had their reasons, and I don't fault them for it.

"You're beautiful," I said, in case no one had before. Like the building, I was caught between what I was and what I would become. I would not have believed it if someone directed those words at me, but maybe, for a moment or a day, it would steal the vigor from my own self-talk, which assured me otherwise.

"Ah, shit," I whispered, catching a glimpse of red spray paint in the fading light. The graffiti was painted on the bricks to the right of a ground-level door. It was about the size of a steering wheel, crude and crafted with an unsteady hand. I hefted the backpack off my shoulder and retrieved my headlamp.

"Strange…" I said, snapping a picture. It was a frowning face, the sadness accentuated by dripping paint, which made the rudimentary eyes appear to weep. The strange part was the antennae. I thought of the cockroach but didn't linger on it. Maybe the artist had not made it inside. The door was trapped behind a dozen sturdy boards that looked several decades newer than the building itself.

How would I get in? I had no tools to destroy, only to document. There were two small windows to what might have been a basement, neither wide enough to allow passage. What if the graffiti was an expression of frustration at being unable to access the inside?

A sigh of a breeze whispered through the tall grass, and what I thought might be chattering field mice turned out to be a rickety fire escape above and to the right of me, responding to the new wind. Its lines blended so well with the building's architecture I failed to notice it. The door it led to was not boarded up, and my headlamp's light was not reflected by an external lock. Maybe it could still be my Everest.

I might have stepped on a banshee for the shriek that erupted from the old metal as I took my first step. Paint disintegrated where my palm gripped the banister. If I was going to die, I would do it attempting to summit my mountain. I took another step, and the volley of shrieks frightened the toads and crickets into silence. The stairs rebelled against my efforts, but they did not buckle. Good thing there was less of me to accommodate – rotting from the inside and all that.

I gripped the handle, pressed the cool metal down with my thumb.

Click

A half-hearted squeak from the hinges, and the door opened for me. My mouth watered, a sudden memory of Grandma's homemade cookies. The air smelled nutty, like almonds or pecans. There were other smells, mildew and wet wood. I nudged the door open with the toe of my boot. A cockroach appeared there, likely falling off its perch along the doorframe. It scaled the laces, and I kicked it free before it could disappear inside the leg of my jeans.

A little flutter in my chest, nothing more. Maybe another explorer turned around here, put off by the infestation, and added the graffiti as a warning before departing.

Inside, my headlamp shone like a cone of moonlight. Paintings on the wall, and that gave me hope this was something other than an abandoned administrative building. The draw to urban exploration was finding a connection with the places people forgot, intentionally or otherwise. Would a cemetery mean as much if there were no bodies, if the headstones were mere tributes? The same is true of buildings. You cannot abandon a thing that was never occupied. You can only walk away from it.

Half a dozen shut doors lined the hallway before a T-split forty or so feet away. Six unopened rooms just for me, and this was only part of one floor. No graffiti. No condoms or beer cans littering the floor. The prior occupants might have left the day before.

CRUNCH

I retreated the step I'd taken and wondered if had stepped on a mustard packet. Then I saw the legs to either side of the stain and understood. I dragged the sole of my boot over the grate of the fire escape, then stepped over the mess on the floor. There were so many rooms to explore. It was like finding my parent's stash of Christmas gifts on a shelf. I could look, but the delayed gratification had its own appeal, preserving the mystery a little while longer.

The doorknob turned easily, the hinges opening silently, but I did not enter the room. I closed the door and walked. The old wood accepted my weight with bursts of violin screeches, the floor slightly spongy underfoot. The next door was also open, as was the door across from it. What I imagined awaited inside the rooms was likely more interesting than the reality. I had seen pictures of other sites, old hospitals with fully equipped operating rooms. Patient records turning to powder. Radiographs of bones long since returned to the earth.

I'd never been so lucky. The filing cabinets I found were always empty, nothing more interesting than a *World's Greatest Dad* mug and a few family pictures with fuzzy edges.

I didn't think to prop the fire exit open, hadn't thought it necessary as a fire exit's sole purpose is to be accessible. It wouldn't make sense for it to lock from the outside. I reached the end of the hallway, where it split in opposite directions, at the same time the door clicked shut. I whipped around, nearly dislodging the headlamp.

The light was broad and failed to reach the fire exit. Still, I backed away until my heel collided with a wall. I liberated the cell phone from my pocket and forgot about it at once.

"Hey!" I shouted, patting my jeans and not feeling the impression of the pepper spray. It was in my backpack, I remembered, as the silhouette shifted in the shadows. It was darker than the door behind it, but the borders of its form were undefined. A man, I guessed, by the approximate height of it, which was equivalent with the top of the doorframe.

Fight or flight. I chose the third, less referenced but perhaps more common response. I froze. Threats cooled in my throat, unspoken. I could only stand, only breathe and wait for him to make his next move.

In a blink, my future assailant was gone. I caught the briefest glimpse, the faintest light reflecting off its... skin? The shudder that passed through me; it was like my muscle fibers were invaded by maggots. Everything twitched, my bones feeling soft as if I might dissolve into a human puddle.

What I saw could not be real. I believed that thought for just a few more seconds as my mind replayed the scene of the *something* as tall as a man skittering up a wall and disappearing like a...

I could not leave through that exit, but I could not stay there with my sanity teetering. My left and right offered equal darkness. I do not recall which I chose, only that after a few paces, my headlamp aimed at the ceiling, I stepped into nothing, and fell.

THE POISON WORMED THROUGH MY BELLY LIKE BLIND VIPERS searching for rats. That's how I pictured it, anyway, gray and slithering, a flicking tongue seeking new organs to infect. It wasn't pain that alerted me to my passenger. It was stirring a bowl of macaroni and cheese with no desire to eat it, the weight loss that inevitably followed. A stomach that felt like a hurricane. Finally, it was a splatter of red in my bathroom sink and a taste of pennies on my tongue.

My body told on itself in many ways, but not through pain. Discomfort, yes. Not pain. Not at first. The pain I felt upon waking, minutes or hours later, was new. I pictured the fracture below the knee of my right leg as a thread made of lightning. My instinct to scream was interrupted by what I thought was a handful of autumn leaves drizzled through a gap in the roof I could not see, now multiple floors above me. But the leaves did not settle. They sprouted legs and walked with a toddler's confidence across my face and neck.

Roaches. Skittering feather-light over my fingers, wedging their slick bodies into the seam between my socks and boots. I could not see then. I could only feel the competing sensations, pain radiating in my leg and an itch that electrified my skin everywhere else. I patted my forehead, flattening a roach but not crushing it in the process. My headlamp dislodged in the fall and my cellphone was no longer in my hand. It was the darkness not of a night under a new moon, but of a rogue planet no longer bound by the gravity of its former sun.

Even that fails to capture it, because that planet would witness the pinprick light of other, distant stars. It was a darkness so thorough I feared my eyes had been lost. I waved a hand in front of my face, flinging roaches in the process. I could not see it, but there was no pain in the sockets, and my eyes felt intact beneath my fingertips.

I patted the ground around my body. Had I fallen through two floors? Maybe I was in the basement I'd glimpsed from the outside. I felt soil between my fingers, soil and the ghost-touches of roach antennae, the cat-claw scrape of their legs over my skin. I sensed a great space around me in the way a person, even blinded, can tell the difference between a closet and a gymnasium without needing to explore.

I could not stand and even shifting my seated position slightly ignited fresh fire in my leg. I gasped and almost inhaled a roach in doing so. Its antennae grazed the roof of my mouth.

So this is how I was going to die. In a pit beneath an abandoned building, slowly drowning in a rising tide of cockroaches. Was it worse than a hospital bed looking at the flowers sent as a stand-in from my mother? I remember the way her posture changed when I told her. How her graceful fingers probed the space above her navel as her mouth fought a grimace. She rejected the idea her daughter was dying or rejected the idea that the genes I inherited from her were the responsible, weak link. My sister created a wall between me and her children, as if my breath might contaminate them. I don't doubt they loved me. I don't doubt they loved themselves more.

I searched the ground for my phone but only felt loamy soil and more roaches. Flipping onto my belly was an effort that doubled my heartrate and ignited the tendrils of pain spreading in my leg. As I inhaled, antennae explored my cheeks and lips. My scream paused in my throat at the thought of a roach skittering into my mouth, lured by its comparative warmth.

My pants were loose, all of them. What was the point in buying smaller sizes when, well, you know. The gap between my pelvis and the denim could have welcomed a cockroach walking upright. Maybe it did. I felt it then, shark teeth tromping through the rough terrain of my pubic hair. Its whisker-like appendages mapped the most sensitive parts of me. I finally screamed.

I did not have the strength to stand but pushed myself into a crawling posture. More roaches beneath my fingers, more soil. A light would not solve my problems, but it would help me understand them. I clambered up what felt like a slight rise in the terrain. Then my hands touched air, and my momentum sent me cartwheeling. I lost control of my legs. Several hard impacts sent aftershocks through my shin. I imagined the break as a fault line between two continents destined for different homes on the globe. My body seized in agony and the darkness beyond it closed in.

THE BEST THING ABOUT DYING IS NOT HAVING TO WONDER. Will it be my heart? Did I eat enough blueberries for my kidneys? Walk or run enough? Are eggs good or bad this week? As a child, I was so afraid of death I prayed to pass in my sleep. As a child! With the rot spreading in my belly, that was a likely scenario, though I no longer prayed.

I came to later. How much later I did not know. The darkness was just as thick. The Universe when all the stars have gone out. The fault line announced itself first, and I reached for my leg on instinct. For a second, I thought my hand was numb. It wasn't. I was holding something, *somethings*, actually, as both hands were occupied. My left hand reported the familiar shape of my cell phone. The right was not so obvious.

The phone was like a miniature sun, the light caged behind a webwork of cracks in the glass. I squinted at my right hand, the object and the feeling of it uniting in my mind. It was an apple. Soft to the touch, my fingertips indenting the skin. It was not fresh but not quite spoiled. My stomach, the time bomb I was unaware I carried, roused from hibernation, quivering into wakefulness as my teeth sank into the mealy flesh.

A roach skittered out of my sleeve, drawn to the scent of the fruit. I blew it off my knuckles and took another bite. Within seconds, I was pulling flecks of flesh off the core, sucking the flavor off the seeds. Little was left but the stem in the end. I flicked that into the darkness, my eyes finally adjusted to the window of light surrounding me.

How had my phone returned to me? Not just in my vicinity but in my hand? Same for the apple. There were a few protein bars in my backpack, wherever that was, but fruit was not a common urbex snack.

It lingered at the border of the light, the gray transition to total darkness. I aimed my phone in time to see its retreat, a cockroach as large as a collie.

"Oh my God," I whispered, scooting backwards with one leg.

The cell phone light was a beacon. Without it, I would be blind. The cockroach did not pursue me as a predator would, hovering outside of the light. Its antennae, like dowsing rods, nearly bridged the gap between us. My breaths came as gasps, but there was no panic in its movements.

"Go!" I yelled or tried to.

I kicked with my good leg, flinging clumps of soil.

"Please…"

The antennae retreated but only for a moment. Out of the darkness, another apple rolled through the spill of light and stopped at my foot.

I don't have much battery left so this will be quick. I've unlocked this phone so that whoever does find it can charge it, turn it on, and find this recording on the home screen. There is no service, so this is all I can do.

My name is Ramona Deeb. I am, or was, an urban explorer. I found a site near Saginaw and, well I didn't get too far in my exploration. I fell through rotted floors and injured myself. I am somewhere beneath the building now. I think I might have been carried away from where I landed. Miles maybe. I don't know.

This place is…infested. Although that's too harsh a word. It's **occupied**. Yeah, I like that better. I don't know if I will make it to the surface. I don't know if I have the strength to try. I think…I think I will go further into the darkness, into the tunnels. There are dozens of them. Isn't that what an explorer does?

I thought this building was my mountain. My Everest. Maybe it was sitting atop it.

Mom, I am sorry for the worry my disappearance will cause you. I am also glad for it. I hate that you began to fear me. I am not contagious, Mom. I am dying. How could you turn your back on that?

I forgive you despite everything. If there is a world beyond this one, I will tell you so someday.

As a child, I prayed that I would die in my sleep. Can you imagine that? A child praying to God to take them in the night so they would be unaware of their peril.

I don't want it now. I want to die doing what I love. I want to die standing.

THE ROACHES CRAWLING OVER MY SKIN REMINED ME I'M alive. Each needle jab of their sharp legs, the tickle of their antennae on my cheeks.

There is so much to explore. A labyrinth of tunnels. The guts of the earth, itself. I am the first person to breathe this air. To touch this soil.

To be this free.

OFFERINGS TO AN OLD GOD

A child every December. A *male* child for the cruelest month, the longest night when only the conifers appear to be living and even the howls of wolves carry the cadence of a eulogy song. The streams clogged with ice, the sun sparking for but a moment between the harsh teeth of the mountains straddling the village, a buffer between its secrets and an outside world that would not understand. It is a bitter time in a harsh land. Each winter solstice, the male babies birthed that year are placed on the doorstep. One will be taken.

"It's *our* way," Papa said, with more than a small measure of pride.

The Briar is a difficult land wedged between a sea that seldom yields its treasure no matter how many hooks and nets are cast into it, and mountains that strain the neck to behold. But the short growing season is bountiful, the game plentiful. And when I was not up to my knees in muck wrangling a hog into its pen, I found it quite beautiful.

Outsiders seldom come to the village, but they do. Desperate men, always. With the rumors of unclaimed women clouding their thoughts.

They ride over perilous roads to reach us and emerge with thorn-lashed cheeks and eyes as wide and hungry as a winter-starved wolf. They are not welcomed with the warmth of some small villages but scrutinized by the steely gazes of unsmiling women beating the dirt out of rugs on a line.

The traveler would notice some men take many wives, and some of the women are attractive by any standard. Maybe it is the hostility in their eyes. Maybe it is the strange mixture of sea air and tree sap. Or something else tugging at a seldom-accessed survival instinct.

What he might forget, retracing his steps with haste, racing the long shadows of the mountain stretching away from the setting sun, is the desperation quivering behind their eyes. So weighted by sorrow they could not imagine another life for themselves. Maybe in the loose, soil-dark locks of these hopeful bachelors they are reminded of a babe trapped in time, forever crying with December air burning in his lungs.

I was nine when my brother, Einar was born. An October baby, he was such a small thing I feared he would not survive the night, whether or not he was taken. The clouds had threatened snow since November and unleashed it the day before the solstice. Mama lay on the floor inside the front door, separated from him by inches that might as well have been miles. She issued hot breath through the small gap beneath the door as if it could warm him against the cold.

Einar cried for a few minutes. Then the world went silent. Papa did not even light a fire on the longest, coldest night of the year. Mama wouldn't permit it. The sound of wood popping and sap sizzling might mask the whisper of Einar's blankets shifting as he was stolen from us.

But there was no theft. And the only sounds we heard were quick sniffles from Mama on the floor and the creak of tree branches bearing the weight of snow, the breath-stealing snap of limbs succumbing. Mama did not sleep that night. I must have drifted, because at the first hint of dawn's light the door was thrown open and a still sleeping Einar retrieved.

A BABY BOY WHOSE NAME I NEVER LEARNED WAS SACRIFICED. While my family celebrated, another mama opened her front door to find a bundle of blankets leaking the warmth of its prior occupant.

An *Old God*, Papa said, though if it was one of ours, he did not share. There were no altars to it, no wooden figures on the mantle. If it had a name, I only heard its corrupted form, slurred by a mourning father too deep into his cup, screamed by a mother who cared not if her wails reached its mountain lair. Papa could not tell me why our gods did not defend us from this terror. When I proposed the question, he appeared to have never considered it.

"Why offer at all?" I asked Papa the year Einar was born. "*We* have swords and fire."

Papa squinted, seemingly trapped between telling me the truth and some softened version of it suitable for my ears.

"They have tried. The men of the village. There are few men for more reasons than the offering. Yes, we know what they say about us in other towns. We devised the tradition to limit competition, to hoard the women for ourselves," Papa said breaking eye contact with me to stare at the liquid swirling in the bottom of his mug. "And every ten years or so some new father or father-to-be will rouse the men of the village to take a stand. Filling them with poisonous words of conquest and dominion. These are not the actions of a man concerned with hoarding women."

"And?" I said.

"Every ten years or so, some red-faced, shield-clanking army ascends the mountain. Five or ten men, it matters not. The war cries fade and there is silence for a while. Then the screaming begins. Here, in the valley, there are a half a dozen or more new widows, and we take care of ours in The Briar."

Maybe in the loose, soil-dark locks of the hopeful bachelors, the women saw not their lost sons but a lost husband who died on a fool's errand.

Papa emptied his mug and reached across the table to muss my hair.

"It is not our concern. This year, at least. Einar was not taken, and Mama is not with child."

I nodded and looked beyond him through the window. The mountain was there, hidden within the fog. The Old God was there, too, a many-eyed black thing according to legend.

"Papa?"

"Yes, dear?"

"What if no boys are born *this* year?"

I WORRIED PAPA BELIEVED I PREDICTED IT. THERE WERE TWO boys born in The Briar the year after Einar, but neither survived to December. This was not unprecedented, and by Autumn Mama began to lose hair from worry. She scrutinized every woman's swollen belly making no mystery of her intentions.

Winter came early and drove Mama inside, where she wore holes in the rugs pacing by the windows with Einar on her hip.

"We'll just leave," Mama said, smiling as if it was the first time she suggested it. "Start a new life somewhere."

Papa shook his head but did not meet her gaze, "You would prefer it be the whole village that suffers, then? You would condemn our brethren to *our* fate? It is the price we pay to live as we do, free from the count's taxes or wars. We die our own way. It is a sacrifice of our own choosing."

Those were the last words they spoke to each other that month. Mama glared at Papa as if *he* was the monster who descended the mountain to steal her child. She pushed Einar away, ripping her breast from his mouth while his belly still rumbled. I understood the feeling. It was like when the hogs I raised from a piglet grew big enough to harvest. I couldn't look at them. I had to pretend they belonged to someone else.

It was quiet that December, and I only had time to think. Papa's words repeated in my head.

A sacrifice of our own choosing.

Was there a truth in his words I did not understand? The offering was a fact of life same as the harvest and the slaughter. It happened without thought, without question.

In one week, Einar would be wrapped in blankets, tight so that he could not wriggle free. He would be left on the doorstep, belly sloshing with a tea to help him sleep through the night. As the only male baby in The Briar, he would be taken. He would be sacrificed to an Old God who lived in the mountain. Forfeiting his life, he would enable The Briar to exist outside of the kingdom's laws and wars for another year.

Einar slept beside me. Though it was cold in the room, we were warm together. His eyelids fluttered in the midst of a dream, soft cooing competing with the rumble from his belly.

It was easy to ignore the hogs, to pretend they belonged to someone else as Papa sharpened the blade that would open their throats. Chunks of meat in a stew could come from any animal. And, soon there would be new hogs, new piglets to fatten with treats hidden in my pockets.

There would never be another Einar even if Mama birthed another son.

Perhaps my thoughts of him pulled him most of the way out of a dream. He wriggled a hand free from his swaddle and it landed in my palm hot as a dying coal. His hands would never create. They would never grasp a sword or plant a seed. And for what?

I found Papa in his chair, a bottle tipped on its side on the small table beside him. He stared at the fire as if attempting to parse meaning from the shifting shapes within. *His* hands were rough and calloused, the nails forever black, veins like green earthworms trapped beneath the skin. *His* hands told a story.

"You will do nothing?" I asked.

He flinched, either from not realizing he was no longer alone or from the sharpness of my words.

"What can I do?" he said, sinking lower into his chair.

"Aye, what can you do?"

The question hung like smoke in the air.

"I cannot best the Old God in combat. I play-fought with swords as a lad, but I've no skill for it today. If we flee, well, others have tried. They do not get far. Briar-folk are loyal, until they aren't. And it would not just be Einar sacrificed but you, me, and yer Ma. Bound and left at the mouth of the cave as penance for missin' the offering."

This was new information. In my short life, there had never been an attempted escape. Papa's reluctance made more sense, but it changed nothing of my resolve. The idea was there, like an acorn buried in the soil waiting for the snow to melt. There was potential, an inkling.

"You would sacrifice yourself in his place. Wouldn't you?"

"Aye, I would."

"If you knew the Old God would accept it, you would offer yourself."

He nodded, eyed the tipped bottle and frowned.

"Then do it. Go to the cave and offer yourself. Bring no weapons."

Papa's rough hands knotted together, and his back bowed as if the thoughts in his mind weighed a hundred pounds each.

"It is certain death," he whispered. "And it might be for naught."

"Might, Papa. Do you wish to live the rest of your days knowing you *might* have saved Einar?"

Papa's eyes shimmered with tears as he lifted his face.

"You wish for me to die?"

I touched his cheek, my thumb wiping a tear, "No, Papa. I wish for you to save our Einar. If it was a bear, you would fight it with your own hands. You would die in the attempt if need be. This is just a different sort."

PAPA SHARED NOTHING OF THE PLAN WITH MAMA. THEY were still not talking but sliding past each other like ghosts. I shared nothing of *my* plan with Papa. He would not have endorsed it and would likely have spent the journey to the Old God's lair glancing behind instead of ahead.

There was snow on the ground, but the sky was dark and full of stars. I held Einar's scent in my lungs as I exited the front door a minute after Papa departed. His prints were half-filled with the moonlight that sparkled off the ice. I could just hear the crunch of his departing steps, and I waited, blowing into my mittens, until all was quiet. If I could hear him, he could also hear me, I reasoned.

The Old God's lair was not at the mountain's summit but somewhere in its middle, below the tree line. There was much space between the boot prints indicating Papa's haste. The air burned in my throat as I shuffled to keep close.

This felt foolish, yes. But it also felt like the only action we could take. I did not know my role in following Papa. I only knew it was my suggestion, and I owned whatever happened to him. A not-small part of me wished to punish the Old God for taking Einar before the offense even occurred. Each time the question of *how* stirred in my mind I bit my lip until the pain was as bright as the summer sun.

Crunch crunch crunch

Up the path we went. I had never climbed on that mountain, though I had many others. I did not want to stumble into the Old God's lair unknowing. The air grew thinner and lighter in my chest as we ascended. It was painful to breathe, and I could not help but imagine my lungs floating free of my chest like a kerchief caught in a wind.

Toward the end I was on my knees, clawing at the ground for purchase so steep was the climb. Papa's prints were grouped closer together here as well.

What did he think of, I wondered. Was he cursing me? Was he afraid? I was just as likely to not survive the night and my only thoughts were of Einar safe in his warm bed.

I nearly gave myself away, stepping out from the trees, which had thinned, and colliding with Papa. I stopped just short, boots crunching and breath trapped in my lungs. He stood with his hands on his hips, a gray-blue silhouette just beyond the mouth of the cave before him. His breath issued around his head like steam from a boiling kettle.

Do you wish to turn back, Papa? Aye, you do. But you will not.

He stepped forward, hands pressing on his knees to ascend the final paces. I timed my movement with his, so that his noise disguised mine. His posture shifted, neck bending, knees bent and ready to run. He shielded his eyes as if it was not darkness he beheld but a bright light.

"Hello?" he called, voice cracking even at a whisper. He cleared his throat and tried again, this time loud enough to make an echo. There was nothing remarkable about this place, a cave similar to dozens I had seen. It felt stagnant. Dead, like the yellowed eyehole of a moldering skull. Was it the wrong cave? Its black mouth swallowed his form, and I realized it might be the last I saw of him.

"Are you there?"

I scurried the remaining distance, finding patches of bare soil padded with discarded pine needles. I crouched beyond the entrance to the cave, eyes straining to catch a glimpse of Papa.

"I say..." he began, then trailed off.

There was a sound from the cave. Sliding and rasping, a scraping of some unknown texture against the walls.

"I...I...am here to..."

Another sound then, like a thrum of struck metal.

Hmmmmm

Papa gasped and retreated a step, the back half of his body now glowing with moonlight.

Hmmm...where...where is your steel?

The voice sounded as if it was formed inside a throat not designed for speech. It was like boulders tumbling down the mountain. It vibrated in my chest, loosened the marrow in my bones.

"I...I have no steel."

Hmmmm...a man...and a girl with no weapons...

"A girl?" Papa said, then turned his head. He could not see me from where he stood, and I held my breath until he faced the darkness again.

"I brought no girl. Only myself."

Hmmmm...so you say. What do you want, man, if not to kill me?

Papa did not answer right away. He could not undo this action, but he still had to speak it into existence.

"My son, Einar, is the only male babe in The Briar. I have come to offer myself in his place. Take me, Old God, and spare my child," he said, then added. "Please."

Hmmm...

Your offer is accepted.

Papa took another step backwards, "It is?"

Yes.

"You will spare my son and take me in his stead?"

Yes.

Papa's back stiffened as if anticipating his end would come at that moment.

"But why, Old God?"

It is what you offered.

Papa scratched his head, "I...don't understand. I...in The Briar...the offering..."

Hmmm...these are your traditions. Not mine. I take what is offered. Your sons. Your men when they come with their steel.

Papa nodded, stepped back into darkness, "But why, Old God?"

Hmmm...I did not demand your sons. It was offered to me long ago. When your kind first came to this valley. A man and a boy with hair like fire entered my cave whispering of sleeping bears. I was in a deep slumber but roused from their racket. Their spears pointed at the darkness, but it was not a bear they found. When the man saw me... hmmmm that is a pleasant memory. His spear fell from his fingers, and he pushed his son toward me. I did not understand his words as I did not know your language then, but I understood his meaning.

"And...and they just kept..."

It is your tradition, not mine. I grow weary of this chatter, man. You have woken me from a blissful dream, and I wish to reclaim it. I accept your bargain, now step forth.

Papa's boots shuffled over the floor of the cave, "Can I ask you a question first?"

Hmmm...you may.

"Are y-you a g-god?"

Hmmm...there are no gods, man.

"Th-then w-what are you?"

I inched forward, eyes hungry for more information, but there was nothing to be seen. I did not want Papa to die even though his death would allow Einar to live. Shame burned in my cheeks when I recalled how small, how diminished he looked asking if I wished for him to die. No. I thought it was the only way.

Could I offer myself instead?

Your understanding of life is a beating heart. It is blood in your veins and air in your lungs. I have no heart. I do not breathe your air. I came to this place while dreaming, floating through the great void beyond the warmth of any sun. There are no gods in the Universe, only chaos. I am but a small part of it.

I do not survive on the flesh of your sons. There is too little to sustain me. What I take from them, you will soon know, is not their meat but something far more precious.

I do not wish to be awake any longer. Close your eyes if you do not wish to die screaming.

"Wait!" I yelled and scrambled free of my hiding place.

"Marit!" Papa cried, rushing out of the darkness and wrapping me in his arms. "You should not be here!"

I looked past him but saw only black. The idea, the acorn buried under snow, broke free of its softened shell and tasted the air.

"The offering. It is our tradition, yes?" I said.

It is.

"It could be something else?"

I am weary of these questions.

"A bigger offering! Bigger and more frequent! You will not have to descend the mountain to claim it. They will come to you," I said, then added, "Imagine how well you will sleep with a full belly. How you will dream."

Hmmm…

Papa's racing heart thudded against my ear. We stared and waited.

What do you propose, child?

The plan took shape as I voiced it. The possibilities were present within me, knowledge of the peculiar nature of our secluded village, the oft-repeated rumors of our disproportionate sexes. I listened to my own echo fade, and Papa held me tighter. Outside the cave, the wind turned the tree branches to rattles.

I wish to dream again. I accept your proposal.

"Thank you! Bless you Old God!" Papa said, shifting me to the cave floor and pulling me toward the entrance.

"Wait! One more question and then we will leave," I said.

"Marit!" Papa barked.

I stood at the border between light and dark.

"The stories in the village of those who claim to have seen you..."

Yeeesssss?

"They said you were a great black creature with many eyes. If you are not that, and you are not a god, what did they see?"

Hmmmm...

A dry scraping sound, raspy, drawing nearer to me. There were lights, faint at first, like the stars I would see only after my eyes had time to adjust. Brighter then, blades reflecting moonlight.

Not eyes. No. They saw the others, those who came before. Their brothers, some. And other kinds still, from worlds barren beneath a blackened star. They saw what they would lose, what they would become when I consumed them. Passengers, awake and static, a part of me, yes. I would drift and dream unaware of the passage of time, and they would exist without living, counting every second, little lights giving structure to my form. They are with me now.

"It *is* like they said," the man slurred, his mug unsteady in his grasp. "The women here. So beautiful and so many."

I feign jealousy, "You said *I* was the most beautiful."

He abandons his mug to grasp my shoulders, "You are! I apologize, my lovely. I am just a little...overwhelmed."

His eyes trace the contours of my face and settle, as they have for the past hour, on my breasts. I do not mind. Nor would any of the women in the tavern, but he chose me.

"You can make it up to me."

His eyes flash back to mine, "How? Anything you ask."

I turn my body away before the drool spilling from the corner of his mouth dribbles onto my chest. He smells of sweat and grime. The journey to get here is not as cumbersome as it was in years past. The road is maintained but still difficult.

"There is a place, not far from here. It will require us to part, though," I say, to which he groans. "A cave. It is sacred to us Briar folk. At the back of the cave there is a waterfall. The water trickles all through the mountain but is only revealed there."

I place the empty mug in his hand.

"Fill this mug with the water. It is special. Magic. You will know it because of the glowing lights. Take no weapons, only this mug. Return it to me and I am yours. For tonight or forever if you prefer."

He glances at the mug as if it is a growth at the end of his fingers, then scans the women in the room.

He has no family, he says. None knew of his journey to The Briar. He is perfect.

"They will require the same of you. It's *our* way," I say, with more than a small measure of pride.

light was obstructed by movement outside. At least they stopped pounding, for the moment.

Throughout the night they pounded. He told her it was Santa's reindeer. She nodded and smiled as she slipped into sleep. He slept beside her, flinching as the mobile home shuddered from the onslaught. It was their refuge, though not their home. In the midst of the chaos, he was glad to have found it. But it was no fortress.

She held the gift in her small hands, her words billowing in frosty clouds, "It says it's from Mommy."

The man blinked tears away. She had not noticed it was *his* handwriting.

"That's wonderful, sweetie."

She looked toward the door, which was crisscrossed with planks.

"Is she coming back?" she asked in a voice as light as a feather.

She proposed the question, in various forms, over the past three weeks. His affirmations lost vigor over time.

"Baby, I promise you'll see her soon, maybe even today."

There was a cracking sound from the bedroom followed by a rippling chorus of inhuman voices. The shadows in the room shifted as the invaders migrated toward the rear of the home.

There were too many. Every other thought in his mind was *there are too many.*

Her head was turned, following the noise of the disturbance.

"Open it, sweetie," he said, dabbing his eyes with his knuckles.

THE FINAL GIFT

He thought they would look like people, but they didn't. Only ever glimpsed through the narrow gaps between the fortifying wooden planks nailed over windows, he could not say what they looked like exactly. But they weren't people.

"Just the one left, Daddy," the little girl said, indicating the final, wrapped gift.

The little plastic Christmas tree bent beneath the weight of the girl's homemade ornaments, mostly tinfoil balls coated with the last of her nail polish. He thought it was the most beautiful Christmas tree he'd ever seen.

"I wonder what it is," he said, eyes darting between his daughter and the wooden planks as the murky dawn

She clenched her mittens between her teeth and tugged them free. The electricity went out two weeks prior, so they made do with winter clothes and blankets. Fortunately, the previous owner of the home subscribed to conspiracy culture, judging by the literature on the bookshelf. Therefore, the home was both remote and well-provisioned.

At first, he made it seem like an adventure. Up in the mountains, eating beef jerky for breakfast, guessing what fruit was hiding in illegibly labeled mason jars. When she slept he listened to emergency broadcasts on the radio and tried to imagine what they looked like, the things now outside his door, now ripping through the brittle walls. In the confusion of their exodus, he had the presence of mind to pack a few gifts on the off chance their adventure endured until Christmas.

She shivered in her Snow White dress, the first gift opened that morning. He draped a blanket over her shoulders and then stood between his daughter and the rising din of snapping wood and shattering glass.

"Don't worry, sweetie. This place is magic, remember? They will never get to you. Open it," he said again, mouth dancing between a smile and a frown.

She nodded and flipped the present over, searching for the seam in the gray light. There was a tremendous crash from behind and her face showed fear for the first time. She was at that tender age where her desire to believe in magic constantly abraded against the reality of life. Maybe the house was not magic. Maybe Santa had not followed her snores to this strange, new home.

"Please open it," he begged, hands secured behind him, back stiffening as the bedroom was breached.

She found the seam and slid her tiny fingers between the paper, breaking the tape.

"I wonder what it could be," she said, voice dreamy, pulled back to the magic again.

Her passions were as varied as her outfits on any given day. In their former life, time was communicated through the piles of clothing strewn about the house. A nightgown represented morning. A leotard and ballet shoes indicated mid-morning. Princess dresses were a sign of the early afternoon. And so, he was only momentarily surprised when her Christmas list to Santa included what she then unwrapped.

"A cuckoo clock!" she said.

"Do you like it?" he asked.

"I love it!"

The house shook as the invaders funneled inside. The locked bedroom door was the only barrier between the two groups.

He hugged his daughter with one arm, tears spilling onto the crown of her head.

"Push the minute hand until just before twelve and you'll see the little bird come out," he said.

She did as she was told and said, "It's probably going to scare me!"

The bedroom door handle rattled. His muscles were toxic with adrenaline.

"Sweetie, you know I love you, right?"

"Of course, Daddy."

"And you know your mommy loves you, too?"

"Yes, Daddy," she said, eyes narrowed in concentration at the clock.

Blood rushed to his face, the sound of his heartbeat drowning out the violence behind him. For a sliver of time, a beat between the flapping of bird wings, it was just the two of them. His little girl in her new dress, wrapped in a blanket, grinning as the bedroom door buckled. His little girl who believed in magic.

"You're the most special girl in the world to me."

"I know, Daddy," she smiled, returning her attention to the clock.

"Just a few seconds now," he said, moving behind her.

The world was only the space between them, that inescapable gravity two souls intertwined. He felt his love for her as if it was produced by its own organ within him.

"Here it comes!" she said as the seconds ticked.

Five

Four

Three

Two

One

The bird popped out, providing coverage for the sound of the safety being clicked. The invaders crawled into the hallway, a strange, coiling gray mass, but he did not look that way.

In his head, he began his own countdown.

Five

Four

Three

Two

One

Pull

THE LAST OF OUR KIND

The night was our playground. In the dark, the desert became something new. By day, the sun shone a harsh spotlight on its frailty, husks of bushes given temporary life by a forgotten monsoon, tumbleweeds shattered into splinters between a wall of tireless wind and the hard-packed earth. When the sun set, trailing pink fingers aimed at the first stars, we staked our claim with whoops and hollers, the wind carving trenches through our hair as we wrestled our bikes over rocks like the broken teeth of fallen gods. This was *our* desert.

Astride my bike, I listened for the crunch of dirt and gravel beneath Victoria's tires. Flashlight tag was not just a game for her. It meant something different. In life, she wasn't good at many things, held back a year in school meaning we only saw her at lunch, a home that wasn't always a safe place. She played to win, to have something no teacher or alcoholic father could take from her. Her light shone for half a second before going dark again.

"Shit!" I whispered, covering my mouth. Victoria was close. She had a predator's instincts, and I was determined to not be easy prey.

Stacy hid behind a boulder, the one she always picked. I knew it and I think Victoria did, too. Gabby could seemingly melt into shadows. We almost never found her except by accident, tripping over a leg she hadn't tucked in far enough. Victoria was looking for me. I was a meaningful challenge.

Too close to pedal. She would hear me and shine a light on my sweaty face, hair pasted to my reddened cheeks. I plucked a rock, warm as a gerbil from basking in the sun all day, from the ground and tossed it at the silhouette of a mesquite. It crashed through the blackened branches and was at once illuminated by Victoria's flashlight.

I pedaled, deliberately riding past a cowering Stacy, hoping to pull Victoria's interest that way. Our eyes met and Stacy pressed a finger to her lips.

I nodded, then filled my lungs with desert air and whooped.

"No fair!" Stacy whined, mounting her bike to search for a new hiding place.

"I hear you, chicas," Victoria said.

Stacy was between us, so I let out another whoop. Some part of me knew more of these nights were behind us than in front. The seams of our group bulged as life and hormones pulled us different directions. Eventually, they would pop, one at a time or catastrophically if Victoria and Stacy's lust for the same boy progressed beyond jokes.

My tires skipped over stones and whipped around thorny bushes. Stacy grunted behind, following the path I created. Victoria would have to tag her first as long as I stayed in front. I smiled. Flashlight tag was a kid's game, but I still liked to win.

I screamed, squeezed my brakes, and skidded to a stop halfway falling off the bike.

Victoria's light tagged my face.

"Gotcha."

"How did…" I began.

"I know where you were goin'? You're not that clever, Eve. You're not goin' deeper into the desert. Too afraid of rattlesnakes and tarantulas."

She wiggled her fingers at me.

"But…"

"And Stacy was behind you. I cut you off. Wasn't that tough to figure out."

She flipped the flashlight off and to my dazzled eyes the world disappeared for a moment.

"I beat you!" Stacy chided between gasps for breath.

Victoria scoffed, "You didn't *win*. You just didn't *lose*."

"Another round?" I said.

"Nothin' else to do," Victoria said, then pivoted her body. "Gabrielle!"

Her voice ricocheted off boulders, diminishing as it spread across the desert.

"Gabby!" I called, hands cupped around my mouth. "New game starting! You have to come out!"

Victoria shook her head, "That girl. She's not even that small. She just…"

"Disappears," Stacy finished.

We spread out, calling for her while covering as much ground as possible. By the time we reached the trailer park, home for both Victoria and Gabby, the frustration in our voices wavered.

"Let's shift to the east some, spread out again," I said.

There was a slight, almost imperceptible fluctuation to the pitch of our shouts, the octave rising on the tail end molding Gabby's name into a question, hinting at the fear chilling the blood in our veins.

"Come on Gabby!" Stacy called.

"It's not funny, chica. You're gonna get us in trouble!" Victoria yelled.

We zigzagged east to west, passing the same mesquite bushes and boulders. Ten minutes. Twenty. We stopped shouting and instead road our bikes in silence, the shadows assembling in the shape of a girl before collapsing into something else upon closer inspection.

"Maybe she went home?" Stacy offered.

Victoria shook her head, "If she did, she's in the dark. No lights on." It was true. From where we stood we could just make out the lines of her trailer, the roof a shade lighter than the night sky behind it.

"What do we do?" Stacy asked.

They both looked to me.

"Let's try one more time."

"And then?" Stacy asked.

"Then…we call the police."

A THIRTEEN-YEAR-OLD GIRL, MISSING FOR LESS THAN TWO hours, was not a priority for local law enforcement. The news barely registered with Gabby's mother, returning home after a fourteen-hour shift. She nodded as I explained how uncharacteristic it was of her daughter, how she always came back. She poured herself a full glass of whiskey and massaged the soles of her feet, eyes drifting away from mine to explore the room.

"I'll leave the door unlocked," she said, then left the kitchen to sit in the living room.

My mother was appropriately aghast, calling the police to demand answers. Belinda, Gabby's mom, wasn't answering the phone.

"Maybe she has a secret boyfriend she's staying with?" Mom suggested.

Unlikely, but nothing else made sense at the time.

On a typical summer night, after flashlight tag, we gathered in my bedroom, Victoria, Stacy, and Gabby. My little brothers would barge in like squealing piglets as we sang Selena songs into a hairbrush. We would chase them away only to be interrupted again minutes later. We played with a Ouija Board crafted from a pizza box, asking the dead to tell us about the cute boys in school. Sometime after midnight sleep would come.

We tried to recreate it in Victoria's house but could not ignore the constant thunder of her father tromping to the refrigerator, the shadow of his boots beneath her door. It didn't feel like a home. It felt like a box placed over something dangerous. Stacy's house was cramped and Gabby's was too sad, pictures of siblings who lived two states away lining the walls, glimpses of normalcy that only existed in her past.

That night I was alone. No girls. No Selena songs. I willed myself to stay awake, ears perked in case Gabby tapped on my window, which she did some nights when her mother stopped at the bar on the way home from work. Alone, the trailer felt too empty, too many closed doors.

I rationalized her disappearance. It was a misunderstanding. A boy, like Mom suggested. It was any number of things. By tomorrow it would make sense. We would gather on my bedroom floor to summon demons with our pizza box Ouija Board, directing them to harass that teacher who called us every Spanish name except our own.

I fell asleep with my face aimed at the stars. Gabby did not tap on my window.

I woke to the shifting of weight on my bed, my feet sinking as my mother sat beside them. She stared at her hands, twisting a tuft of tissue between slow-motion fingers. Her face was a two-tone map, bronze and pink, patches of the latter splattered on her cheeks and climbing her neck toward her jaw.

"Mom?"

She sighed.

"They found her."

I sat up. That was good news, why the tears?

"Where is she?"

Mom shook her head, filled her lungs and hesitated to speak the words building pressure in her chest.

"Mom?"

"They, uh, found where she was attacked."

"Attacked?"

Mom nodded, "Probably a mile-and-a-half from where you were playing."

"She's okay, though? Can I see her?"

Mom tore her gaze away from the knotted tissue. This was the hard part. Whatever she was about to say would be the worst thing she'd ever told me.

"There was a lot of blood, Eve. They…they didn't find her body, but there was so much blood. She couldn't have survived."

I didn't feel the hand she placed on my knee. Couldn't have survived? It didn't make sense.

"I'm so sorry, sweetie."

Mom stroked my arm.

"No. No, you said they didn't find her. She could-"

Mom smiled as she shook her head. There was no joy in it. All other emotions were simply exhausted. Gabby was a fixture in our house, the quiet, polite girl who said *thank you* for the smallest gesture, a glass of Sunny Delight or a bowl of microwaved Frito pie.

"I want to go. I want to see for myself."

Mom shook her head again. The mattress springs mouse-squeaked as she stood.

"It's a crime scene, sweetie. There was an old campsite. He must have snatched her while you were playing. Took her there and…"

She walked baby steps to my door and stood with her hand braced on the doorframe.

"I hope they find him. Whoever did it," she said, then turned to look at me. "Come out when you're ready. I'm so, so sorry."

VICTORIA AND I WATCHED FROM THE ROOF OF HER TRAILER, glints of light reflected off distant badges, fuzzy caterpillar shapes of men warped by heat and distance. Mom was with Belinda, answering the door to accept casseroles and plastic grocery bags brimming with tinfoil-wrapped tamales.

"What do you think happened?" Victoria asked.

"Guess it's like they said. She got too far away, and someone took her. I don't want to guess what happened at the campsite."

"We would have heard."

I shrugged, "Maybe. What if he knocked her out first? I mean, we aren't exactly quiet when we play."

What if one of my *whoops* had masked the sound of her abduction? My skin prickled from something other than the heat, hair stiffening like seedlings straining for sunlight.

"I can't believe it," Victoria mumbled.

The expression was like a tennis ball volleyed back and forth between us. It meant nothing, had become our default setting when the silence persisted too long.

"It could have been us," I said.

Victoria nodded and began to pick at the frayed threads sprouting from her shoelaces. She needed a new pair. Gabby wore the same size, and she no longer needed shoes.

I shook my head as if attempting to dislodge the thought from my brain.

"I didn't wanna say it, but I was thinking the same thing," Victoria said.

DAYS PASSED. THE SITE WAS CLEARED, THE OLD TENT AND whatever else they found out there. A stream of onlookers visited what was left, the morbidly curious, classmates, and relatives. Her father and siblings only stayed for a day, appearing much older than the pictures on the walls of Gabby's home.

We brought flowers. Stacy left her Selena tape next to the stone mottled with Gabby's blood. I placed a note beside it but pocketed it before we left. I didn't want anyone else to read it. Victoria lingered at the outskirts, thumbs hooked in her beltloops, eyes landing anywhere other than where we stood.

We were no longer free to roam the desert. Curfews hung over our heads, even Victoria, whose father eased off the bottle as Gabby's friends, relatives, and law enforcement swarmed the trailer park. My mother attempted to soften the blow of our interrupted summer by offering herself as a taxi.

Anywhere you want to go Mom said.

We weren't fit to be in public, though, and so mostly huddled in my room, listening to the whisper of her footsteps as she lingered outside the door. I unfolded and refolded the note I'd written, wondering what I should do with it.

"Maybe we could try to contact her?" Stacy said, nodding at the wrinkled pizza box under my bed.

Victoria shot her a look, ending the conversation.

We could think of nothing to discuss beyond Gabby and what might have happened to her. Where was her body? What was *he* doing to it? Were *we* next?

This was a couple of summers before the world would be flooded with AOL trial discs. We were aware the Internet was a thing but had no access to it. That was probably for the best. Had we discovered the true crime backwaters of the early Internet we would have lost what little remained of our childhoods.

The girls were returned to their homes before nightfall, and I was left to chew on the questions we proposed but could not answer. Again, I propped my head on the pillow so I could see out the window. My father lost his battle against the west Texas sun weeks prior, our lawn transformed into a fossil of its former self. I stared at it through a tide of brimming tears, recalling the nights I woke to find her standing there, awaiting an invitation. I would crack the window, grab her by the forearms and hoist her inside.

Yes, her mother did drink, but Gabby never wore long sleeves during the summer, sunglasses indoors like Victoria. It was not fear that inspired her midnight sojourns. It was sadness.

"I feel like a ghost," she told me one night. "Like I'm haunting my own home, you know? Walking the halls, peeking into their rooms. I-I wish they were empty. I wish their stuff was gone. Even when they come back it's not the same. They have a whole life I'm not part of. Why? Why did it happen this way?"

In my house she was a guest, not a ghost.

I was awake, I think, on the fringes of a dream dragging me toward sleep when I heard the familiar squeal of the gate's latch. My backyard appeared no different, clusters of brittle grass floating on a dirt sea, the bane of my father's life. Somehow, they assembled themselves into the shape of a girl, just like the shadowed foliage during flashlight tag.

It was Gabby.

I missed her so much I conjured her, standing next to the bike she abandoned in the desert when she was taken. She waved. I sat up in bed, shaking the comforter free from my shoulders.

There was something different about her eyes. They glowed like pennies in the sun, like deer caught in headlights.

"Gabby?"

I wrenched the window open with such force it rebounded off the top of the frame.

She waved again, then walked her bike away, disappearing around the corner of the house.

My muscles trembled with potential, as if they could move mountains. But for a moment all I could do was stand, mind warring with the memory of Gabby's blood, blackened on the boulder in the desert, and the image of her standing in my backyard.

"It wasn't real," I whispered as I wedged my feet into a pair of sneakers by my door.

There were landmines in the floorboards between my room and the front door, trapped gunshots that would surely wake my mother. She had taken to roaming the house at night to check the locks. That I did not encounter her in the hallway was a minor miracle.

With ghost-light touches, I padded past her bedroom and into the living room.

What am I doing? Sneaking out of the house at midnight days after Gabby was abducted probably less than fifty feet from me and then murdered? Mom will shit a brick if she checks on me and I'm not there.

I exited via the backyard door, pocketing the key after locking it.

It's not real, anyway. You'll be back in bed in a minute.

The gate was open, though, and in the sparse patches of grass there was an unmistakable, tire-width line. A jawbreaker-sized lump sprouted roots in my throat. I swallowed, untangled my bike from those of my brothers, and followed the depression in the grass.

She was a diminishing wisp on the sidewalk, hair like a paintbrush fanned across her shoulders. Gabby, or her ghost, neared the end of the street. I clamped a hand over my mouth to stop from screaming her name.

Where are you going?

I mounted my bike, unleashed the strength to move mountains on my pedals. Within seconds I was flying, a wolf with the scent of blood in its nostrils. Her disappearance was a pivot point in my life, an event I would forever describe as *before* and *after*. My trajectory without her was unknown to me. Gabby and I were supposed to graduate together. Four years of high school and we could put our quaint desert life in the rearview.

I took a right. Too hard. Tires skipped and skidded, the bike fighting me like an untamed bronco.

There she was, one block ahead.

"Gabby!"

My attempt to yell came out library-quiet, aching lungs focused on powering my legs.

Where are you taking me?

She turned left, riding out of the neighborhood. It was the same path we took to the trailer park and the desert beyond it. Was she leading me back to the site of her death? It was definitely something a ghost, not a living person, would do. The jawbreaker I previously swallowed reformed in my throat.

I pedaled furiously, as if I was trying to destroy my bike rather than ride it, but I came no closer to her. She entered the trailer park and turned toward her home. I flew past twenty seconds later and saw Belinda in the living room, slumped on the couch with an open bottle in her lap. Her nightshirt was damp with spilled liquor.

Gabby did not even turn her direction. Her hair, lifted by desert wind, streamed behind, a patch of quivering black against the gray terrain. Days ago, we played flashlight tag here, not knowing it would be the last time.

The memorial display, a wreath of white roses, glowed faintly to our right. She ignored it as well. She ignored my shouts, breathless as they were, and led me to the mesa which, in daylight, cast a long shadow that fell just shy of the trailer park.

"Gabby! Wha-where were you?" I said, walking my bike the remaining ten yards between us. She was real, no spectral fog in the shape of a girl. But she was also different. I propped my bike on its stand but did not leave it. The feeling was born deep in my belly, a mass of sun-warmed worms creating space between my organs.

"Gabby?"

There was a boulder beside her, one I did not recall from our occasional visits to the mesa. She lifted her left arm and pointed to a black gash in the sediment, roughly the same size and shape as the boulder. Then she walked inside.

"Gabby, why aren't you saying anything?"

I aimed the flashlight at the narrow chasm.

"Come in," she said in a flat voice.

"I'm scared."

"I'm not going to hurt you. I need to show you something."

From where I stood, I could just make out the lights of the trailer park. How long had I been gone? I imagined my mother cracking the door to my room to find my comforter on the floor.

"Please," Gabby whispered.

I approached the gap. How had I never noticed it before? And then screamed, as my light peeled the shadows from the atrocity just inside. I turned to run, but Gabby yelled for me to stop.

"Eve! Please! Let me explain."

I stopped, heart trembling in a spiderweb.

She tugged my shirt, pulling me into the cave. I stepped around the severed legs, gagging at the fish-belly white feet with untamed, leathery nails.

I seethed, "Your hands are like ice!"

Gabby nodded. I lifted the flashlight, but she pressed my arm down.

"Not yet. Let me explain first."

"Okay."

Her eyes shined like mirrors in a mostly darkened house.

"He took me," she said, pointing to the legs. "While we were playing. It was so fast. He took me away from you. I could hear you and the girls. For a while.

Then, he set me down and told me not to scream. I didn't have a choice. I know that now.

He said he was sorry. He hadn't planned to do it. He couldn't help himself. He was afraid, said he was the last, that he had been alone for so long. He was afraid of what would happen to him, didn't think he could do it…"

She dropped her gaze, looked to the side for a moment.

"He didn't think he could do it *empty*. I didn't know what he meant, but it makes sense now."

I shook my head. None of it made sense to me.

"He lunged at me, bit my neck…and started drinking. Kind of a blur after that."

"What?"

I took a step backward, and Gabby placed a hand on my shoulder, stopping me.

"I think he meant to drain me. To kill me. But he was old and clumsy. He left me and came here. And that," she said, pointing again. "Is what the sun did to him."

"Gabby…you're not…"

"I might not have believed it either. They're just stories, right? Look."

She moved aside and gestured for me to pass. I did and aimed the flashlight. The cave was like a beehive, half-circles carved into the earth, maybe twenty in total.

"What are they?" I asked.

"Look."

I walked to the nearest divot and shone my light.

"Oh my God!"

Before I could turn away, Gabby grasped my wrist and shone the light on the skeleton's skull.

"Look," she said again.

Paper skin clung to the cheeks like bleached corn flakes. A few wisps of ebon hair sprouted from an island of shriveled flesh at the crown of the head. But, in the moment, I only saw the teeth.

"Some are…fresher."

I moved the beam around the room, light flaring off black silk hair as glossy as my father's dress shoes.

"Gabby, I-I…this is a lot to take in."

She nodded, "I thought about just walking out into the sun. Ending it before it begins, you know? But I'm not ready. I don't *feel* like a monster," she said, then tapped her head. "In here."

"What can I do?"

Instead of answering, she walked past me and sidestepped the legs near the entrance to the cave.

"It looks different, now. Brighter. I can see these little red lights everywhere. Hearts beating in tiny chests. There's a lot more than you would think. A coyote just fifty feet away from us over there," she pointed. "An owl over there."

"Gabby?"

"I need blood. I tried with an animal and it…it's not the same. Some things I just *know* now."

She looked at me, a smile forming and collapsing on her face.

"I'm still me. I'm still Gabby."

I nodded and didn't shy away as she held my hand.

"Okay. I'll help."

THE SLEEPOVER WAS OUR COVER. TO AVOID BEING PEPPERED with questions I said nothing until my parents had been in bed for an hour. Neither girl was hesitant to accompany me when I mentioned it was about Gabby.

"Why the cup and knife?" Victoria asked as we pedaled toward the mesa.

I didn't answer.

"SO, YOU NEED OUR BLOOD?" STACY SAID.

Gabby sat on the boulder, her silver dollar eyes witness to a version of the desert I could not perceive.

"Yes. I'm figuring this out on my own. I-I just have my instincts to go on. He was dead when I got here, didn't leave any notes," she said with a chuckle. "I probably would have been…dead I mean, but I hadn't transitioned fully."

Victoria emerged from the cave and turned off the flashlight, "Desert vampires. Freaking desert vampires."

"And you need our blood?" Stacy said crossing her arms.

Gabby nodded.

"It's just-just tough to believe, you know? Like, all the evidence is there. But I'd almost believe it was a joke first. Like this was all a prank," Stacy said.

Gabby nodded again, then stood on the boulder.

"I wonder how long they were hiding in there, how many times we walked right up to this rock not knowing what was on the other side of it?" Gabby said.

"I live like, half a mile from here, chica. I don't wanna think about it," Victoria said.

Stacy shook her head, "It can't be real. There's…"

As she trailed off, I turned to see what had stolen her attention.

Gabby hovered about eight feet above the boulder, arms aloft.

"I can't do it for long. I'm too weak," she said, then descended.

Stacy and Victoria looked from Gabby to me. I had already made up my mind. I picked up the knife.

"I'll go first."

IN BED THAT NIGHT, MY HEART WAS SETTLED KNOWING GABBY was still around even if she wasn't technically alive. She flew us, like Superman cradling Lois Lane, to the top of the mesa where we sat, legs dangling over the precipice.

At times, it felt normal. We talked about boys, the school year to come.

For Gabby there would be no boys in her future, no school. For Gabby there would be only blood.

And among us girls, we did not have enough of it.

As I drifted to sleep, I pictured Gabby licking her crimson mustache, locking eyes with me and saying, "More."

We gave what we could but less than she needed. Stacy stopped answering the phone. Victoria's father found the self-inflicted wounds on her arms and sent her to live with an aunt in El Paso. This was far from a noble gesture, one rooted in his fear that what he perceived as self-harm would raise red flags about him.

As summer neared its end, it was just us. We sat on the mesa, moonlit clouds like tattered flags snuffing out stars overhead.

"I have to go back to school next week. I can't come out here like this," I said.

Gabby nodded, "I know. Thank you for sticking around as long as you have. I-I'm afraid of what I'm going to have to do now."

She draped her thin, cold fingers over mine. There was less of her, less substance to her. She was dying in a way I could not understand.

"How can I do monstrous things without becoming a monster?" she asked.

"Well, you're sitting here with me. Every instinct tells you to feed, right? You need it. I can tell.

But you don't do it. You still have a choice. You have to feed, but you get to pick who. I can think of a few people who would be better off dead," I said, and we both looked toward Victoria's darkened trailer.

"I guess you're right."

The following night, Gabby did not come to my window. By the next week I was so involved in school I stopped looking for her. The disappearances began in September. Always at night. Always someone who wasn't really missed. By December, they stopped. A small town in New Mexico lost track of half a dozen scoundrels through the winter.

On my birthday, I found a *Land of Enchantment* keychain on my windowsill. The next year there was a *Big Sky Country* postcard, which coincided with a plague of miscreant vanishings in the state.

I reciprocated, mostly with notes. I saw her a few times, a waifish specter with that same, sheepish wave.

The birthday gifts followed me to Colorado, where I moved after college. Gabby faded to the background of my thoughts, but she was always there, a memory waiting to be jostled by a Selena song on the radio.

MY HUSBAND DIED NEVER KNOWING THAT PART OF MY LIFE. My daughter, who was in the car with him, would have been too young to understand.

It was not a secret. It was just too unbelievable to share.

I HAVE WAITED ALL NIGHT FOR HER. ALTHOUGH SHE DOES come by randomly, she *always* visits on my birthday.

This year, I find it hard to celebrate. The note I left on the windowsill is not a recap of my recent past. It's an invitation.

I answer the door, the knock barely audible above the rushing of blood in my ears.

She hasn't aged since the night she was attacked, hair the same sleek curtain. Mine is streaked with silver. She could pass for my daughter.

"Can I come in?"

I smile, "Is that a real thing?"

She shrugs.

"Yes, come in."

We sit in the living room and for a time say nothing. Their pictures are on the wall, the silence of their absence filling the space between us.

"Are you sure? It's not like what you think."

"How so?"

She sighs, "The hunger. It only grows."

I nod, "You've been busy."

"You noticed?" she says, smiling.

"Idaho in December? Utah a couple of months before?"

She smiles again.

"I wrote a letter to you, meant to leave it at your memorial site, but I didn't. I kept it. It was too personal, probably overly dramatic, but I was just a kid."

"Yeah?"

"I wrote about how I imagined we would be together forever. In some way. Remember when you used to visit me at night? Before?"

She nods.

"I needed that as much as you."

She nods again.

I hook a finger inside my collar and tug.

"Does it hurt?" I ask.

Gabby stands, fangs descending, "You won't remember."

ONLY EVER NIGHT

Exhausted, belly taut and aching, Derek dreamed of the carnival the moment his head hit the pillow. Blinking lights and swirling colors, so vivid compared to the landscape beyond his front door. He smacked his lips, tongue searching the corners for the residue of fried dough dusted with sugar. It was a night to forget the crops wilted in the fields, the milk cow, whose calf was stillborn with eyes like pond water. He burned through his few pennies quicker than planned, but even with his money spent it was better. No thoughts of the farm, of earth hard enough to snap a shovel in half.

He roused with calliope music still tinkling in his ears, children laughing. He heard his father's heavy footsteps elsewhere in the house but thought it a mistake, a final tendril of the dream slipping silently into the dark. His eyes fell to the window, the curtains partially drawn with a thin rectangle of black between them. There was no murky morning light leaking through, and so Derek turned over and fell back into dreams.

Not the carnival this time. He would not be so lucky. And the dream had only minutes to take root before new sounds wrestled him out of sleep. The thump of a coffee mug placed on the kitchen table. Derek yawned and stretched, head cocked curiously at the window. It was still night, the visible portion of the window unchanged.

Wilma snored, an abrupt bark like a puppy with a burr in its paw. Her back was to him, and her hair, the same copper red as the deer that meandered through their dying fields, appeared black in the dark. There was only one clock in the house, and it rested on the mantle above the fireplace, but Derek knew it was later in the morning than it seemed.

"Wilma!" Derek whispered.

She flinched but did not wake.

"Wilma, wake up!" Derek said.

Her snore tapered off and she flipped onto her back. Derek swiveled his legs of the bed and padded to her bed, dusty wooden floors squeaking beneath him. A scrape of chair legs from the kitchen, his mother and father speaking as if they did not want the children to overhear their words.

Derek touched Wilma's shoulder.

"Wilma, are you awake?"

She blinked and stared at the ceiling.

"Hey, somethin's going on."

She licked her lips and mumbled, "What?"

Derek nodded toward the window.

"It's dark outside."

Wilma followed his gaze to the window, "So?"

"Somethin's going on. Let's go," he said, and walked to the door.

She grumbled as if he'd asked her to haul a bag of feed to the barn. But she followed behind as he stepped into the hall. Their parent's voices volleyed back and forth, a steady drone from their father contradicted by their mother's wavering tone edging near panic. The pair tip-toed into the living room, hands braced against the wall to relieve some of their weight, avert the floorboard squeal that might give them away. Their parents stood in the doorway and stared out at the lawn. The words were louder, but no clearer.

Derek glanced at the clock and nudged Wilma.

"What?" she whispered.

He pointed to the clock. At seven years old she was old enough both to tell time and to understand it was still dark when it shouldn't be.

"We're late for school," she said.

"I don't know if that matters right now."

They crossed the living room, no longer masking the sound of their movement. It did not matter. Their parents were lost in their own confusion.

"...make a lick of sense. I suppose I should go to town."

Their mother stiffened at the suggestion.

"Are you sure? What if something bad's happening?"

"Only one way to find out," he said, turning and catching sight of the children. A false smile twitched at the corners of his mouth.

"What is it, Dad?" Derek asked.

Daryl shook his head, "Don't rightly know, son. Clock's not wrong, that's for sure. Been waitin' for sunrise for a couple hours now."

"Are we safe?" Wilma squeaked, face half-hidden behind her brother's shoulder

Her mother kneeled so she was eye-level. She spread her arms and Wilma walked into the embrace.

"We will be, baby."

Derek joined his father on the porch. Inside, Wilma's attention was redirected to breakfast, her favorite meal of the day. Only a few hens laid eggs anymore, and about half of those were bad, the shells oyster gray and soft. Darlene closed the curtains above the wash basin and hoped Wilma might forget about the darkness.

"What do you make of it?" Derek asked.

Despite the lack of protein in his diet, and that mostly from beans, he had grown nearly as tall as Daryl that year. They both stared at the field, silhouettes of cornstalks blistered by the sun shuddering in the breeze.

"I don't know, son. I do think we ought to go to town and see what others are sayin'. Maybe there's a reason for it."

"Should we turn on the radio?"

The moon was nearly full, the topography masked by its brightness. Daryl squinted. There was something different, something off he sensed but could not put into words. As he approached understanding a scream pulled him back inside.

"Daryl?"

Darlene held an egg in her hand, part of an egg, he realized. It wasn't gray like the bad ones, but the shape was wrong. She held it away from her as if it was a coiled snake. Her hand trembled, the egg rocked back and forth across her palm. It was half an egg, a little less, but the shell was still intact.

It was disappearing.

"Daryl?" she cried.

He plucked the egg from her hand and held its dwindling form between his thumb and forefinger. Over the course of ten seconds, his fingers came closer and closer together as the egg evaporated. Swallowed by a ghost. There was no sound. There were no errant particles floating about.

His thumb and forefinger touched. The egg was gone.

THEY PACKED INTO THE OLD FORD NOT BOTHERING TO change out of their sleeping attire. Darlene hummed a church hymn and tapped her shoe on the floorboard, refusing to let her mind settle. The children sat in silence, Wilma burrowed into her brother's side like a suckling piglet. The world beyond his window was a haze, the desolation of neighboring farms like thin pillars of ash. He wrestled with the reality of a disappearing egg, wondered how it was connected to the absence of daylight. It had to be.

"It's okay," Daryl said once a minute or so, the only words spoken. He hoped the problem was local to the house, to his farm, but it didn't feel that way. The air was different, how it transmitted sound. It was like his ears were plugged with cotton. Speaking the words was not for the benefit of his family. If an egg could be lost, why not his hearing?

The handful of streetlamps in their small town struggled to repel the darkness. In the weak light they conjured, however, the shreds of Daryl's hopes turned to cinders. Families clogged the streets, migrating toward the town center like moths to the last candle in a darkened room. The crowd outside the jail likely represented half the county. Judging by the attire, each had come in a hurry.

"Here's good," Daryl said. The Ford was parked and abandoned as if the engine had caught fire.

"I'm telling you, Jack, it ain't a police matter," the sheriff said.

He held his hands up as the crowd responded with murmured jeers.

"Then what sort of matter is it?" the man, Jack, said.

"I can't control the weather. What you want me to do, shoot the moon?"

"Can't you call someone? Can't you ask Denver about it?"

Another murmur rippled through the crowd.

The sheriff lowered his hands but glanced at his watch as he did. Two hours prior, he was convinced the watch was broken. Though he accepted this was not true, he still expected a different result. Then he could dismiss this as a dream, the townsfolk as unfortunate actors within. He looked down the street, over the heads of the crowd. No sun that direction. Not even the snow-tipped fangs of the mountains were visible.

"You're not going to do *anything?*" a new voice added.

The sheriff removed his hat to run his fingers through his hair. The crowd sensed weakness in his hesitation, a direction for their angst.

"What're you not tellin' us?" Jack asked.

Daryl weaved his way to the front of the crowd. He caught the final few months of Europe's *Great War*. A few skirmishes, but mostly cleaning up the mess left behind by other armies. He learned more about humanity there than in his lifetime before it. How quick a collection of scared people could turn carnivorous.

"Bill, what is it? What do you know?" Daryl asked, one hand gripping the man's shoulder.

The sheriff sighed and nodded for a moment, deciding how much of the truth he should reveal.

"Can't call anyone. Phones don't work. Radios are only picking up static."

He swallowed hard.

"That it, Bill? There somethin' else?" Daryl asked.

The sheriff stared at his boots, lips rolled into a thin line.

"I sent Hank and Roger out. Dispatched 'em over to Cheyenne Wells."

"Yeah? What they find?"

Sheriff Bill shook his head, "I don't think they made it. Had a little back and forth over the radio, then they stopped answering. Been over an hour now. Only static."

Jack faded into the crowd whispering, "Only static?"

Without a shepherd to guide their anger, the town's mood shifted. The fear repurposed as anger stimulated old instincts. With no discussion, the crowd navigated a block down the street to the church. It was Friday, at least it should have been, but they filed in and took their normal places in the pews as if it was Sunday morning. Pastor John stood at the lectern scribbling notes in the margins of his bible.

Lantern light cut flickering shapes from darkness. A push and pull of shadows. On a typical Sunday morning there was enough light from outside the lanterns were not needed. On a typical Sunday morning there was music, the smell of pies in the fellowship hall wafting through the pews.

Pastor John dabbed his nose with a handkerchief and began to read. He selected several passages about the Lord being a light in the darkness, about the great mysteries of the Universe, how what was unknowable would be known in time. A handful of heads nodded, but most were still, aimed at the windows that would reveal the true nature of their God. Source of miracles or a fraud. More townsfolk filed in and lingered in the back of the room. Pastor John acknowledged them with a head nod and returned to the verses.

"That's all good, John, but what are we supposed to do? Does it say anything about that?" a man asked.

"Now hold on, Sam, I'm trying to be a comfort here, provide some perspective," Pastor John said, then flipped to a new passage. His finger twitched and smeared the note he'd written a minute before.

"So, you don't know?" Sam said.

He was seated in the front pew, burly arms crossed over a barrel chest.

"What's happening? No, the Bible doesn't talk about what's happening in Colorado in 1936. I'm doin' my best. *You* came to *me*," Pastor John replied, holding the man's gaze until Sam swallowed and glanced at a window. "The sun has not risen. What does that mean fo-"

"It's not just the sun! There's things out there! I saw 'em in the field like...like..." Sam trailed off.

"I saw one too!" a voice called, with several corroborating.

Pastor John flipped through the bible, his unsteady fingers tearing the delicate paper. Before he could speak, the rear doors flew open. Screams, a stampede of bodies twisting away from the figure standing in a silver rectangle of moonlight. Women hugged children to their sides and more than one man reached for a gun he had not brought.

"It's alright. It's okay," John said, recognizing the girl. "She's one of us."

Her name was Beth, an unwed teen mother. The status that might have been a stain in another small town, but not for her. The town rallied around her, pitching in with little Daisy when they could. Some mornings, she walked out her front door to find bottles of milk, fresh-baked bread still warm from the oven. In lean times, this was no small sacrifice.

Her tongue stumbled over the words she wished to speak. What came out was something like a calf's bleat, a warbling keen in the shape of a name.

She pressed the bundle, the pink swaddling blanket, to her breast. Her knuckles threatened to split the skin, eyes wild with fear as if there were rattlesnakes hidden in the fabric.

"Daisy," she said, as the blanket unraveled.

It pooled at her feet, and she stared at her empty hands not understanding.

"Oh," she piped, then collapsed with a muffled WHUMP.

Daryl sprang to his feet, as did a few others. There were calls to lift her legs and some shouts from the front pew about preserving her dignity.

"Quiet!" Daryl barked, folding the swaddling blanket into a pillow he slipped beneath her head.

Beth roused within seconds and was momentarily confused at the collection of leering faces.

"Where is she?"

Daryl shook his head.

Like the others, Beth waited for a sunrise that did not come. She walked a quarter mile to her nearest neighbor, found the lights on but no one home.

"Daisy was asleep. I'm so used to carryin' her it sometimes feels like carryin' nothin'. I headed to town. Didn't know what else to do. I guess I wasn't even thinkin' about Daisy. I was so scared. Couple minutes ago I stopped to move her to my other shoulder and...that's when..."

"It's okay," Daryl said, offering a handkerchief.

"She was gone. Just gone."

Pastor John leaned over the lectern, eyes dancing over the text in front of him. He searched the passages for something relevant, something to steady the hearts of his restless flock even for a moment. The floorboards popped as a family of seven exited their pew, the father shouldering past the men loitering over Beth.

"Outta my way. Fuckin' useless this is."

Murmurs. Looks exchanged. A few loners peeled themselves off the walls and headed for the open door.

Pastor John slammed the bible shut.

WHAM

"I could make up something about the end times. This fits, doesn't it? But that would be for me, not you. I could fill you with hope, fill your cups to overflowing. I have that power. But I am not that man. On a night like this, a day if we're going by the clock and not what's outside the window, I would not choose the path taking you away from God. Maybe we're being tested. He tested others. Why not you? Why not me? I suggest you go to where you feel safe, if there is such a place. If praying helps your heart then do that, too."

Pastor John left the Bible on the pulpit and parted the curtains hiding the door to his office. As he did, the walls echoed with fresh screams.

Sam was out of his seat and dancing in the aisle, arms thrashing, uncoordinated like a child's marionette. For a moment, Derek thought he'd been possessed by the Spirit. He hadn't seen it in that church but heard about it happening in the revival tents that set up on the outskirts of town. In the low light it was difficult to make out precisely what the man was doing, twirling in his overalls, eyes big like he was stepping on nails.

Well, not exactly something. He was looking at nothing.

"Dad?" Derek whispered.

Daryl's gaze was fixed on the man, who stared at the stumps of his arms.

"I can still feel 'em!" Sam screamed. "I can feel my fingers!"

Inch by inch they disappeared, the skin and bone retreating like a wave returning from its flirtation with the shore.

"Oh my God! I can still feel 'em!"

Sam turned his face away as if the stumps were on fire.

His scream was awful, like the cow calling for its dead calf long after the dogs had coaxed the marrow from its bones. After a week of it, Daryl wanted to put her down, but they needed the milk.

Sam's torso disintegrated next, beginning at the shoulders. He stood on tiptoe as if trying to keep his head above water. The crowd of gawkers, perhaps fearing the phenomenon was contagious, fled like a spooked herd.

"Tell Maddie I lov-"

His daughter was not present to hear the declaration, a selfless gesture in the final second of a brutal man's life. He was gone. In the place where the man stood there were only confused impressions of his boots on the carpet.

"I THINK I KNOW WHAT IT IS, DAD," DEREK SAID.

"What's that?"

Daryl passed the beer to his son. It was warm and Derek didn't care much for the taste, but it seemed important to his father, this moment between them. The girls were inside using the last of their sugar to bake cookies.

"The moon. It's further away," Derek said.

It was true, not just that the moon was smaller, but that it appeared further away.

"It's like were fading. Drifting." Daryl said.

"Where do you think they go?" Derek asked.

Daryl shook his head, reclaimed the beer, and finished it with one gulp.

"I don't know, son. I hope the Lord doesn't make me find out."

Under a typical full moon most of the cornfield facing the house was visible. Illuminated only by the light from the kitchen, it was then a gray blur, and Derek could no longer see the outline of the scarecrow he erected the previous summer. Maybe that was gone, too.

"Dad, what's that?" Derek said, pointing.

Daryl set the beer on the step and followed the direction of his son's finger. There was a faint, white glow amid the gray of the cornfield. It slithered through the stalks, its shape shrinking and growing. Daryl shuddered and dabbed the sweat dappling his brow.

"I don't know son. Let's check on the girls."

After Daryl closed front door, he stayed there for a minute, peering through its small circular window. He then locked the door and walked quickly to his bedroom, returning with the shotgun he kept propped against the wall.

The cookies were slightly undercooked, rushed with the unspoken worry what happened to Sam might happen to one of them. The family sat in the living room around a crackling fireplace, stealing small bites and dancing around the words they wished to say but couldn't.

"They're real good," Derek said. "Thanks Mama."

"I helped!" Wilma whined.

"Soon you'll be able to make them without the recipe card..." Darlene said, her smile leveling to a flat line as her thoughts chased the idea down an uncomfortable path. What if there was no *soon*? What if one or all of them were *disappeared* before then?

In five-minute intervals, Daryl left his chair to pull back the curtains and gaze into the darkness, the shotgun never leaving his hand. The clock's hour hand indicated eight, but none knew for sure if this was morning or dusk. How long had they been awake? How much time passed?

"Daddy, what happens if we disappear?" Wilma asked. "Like the moon and stars?"

She was curled into a ball on the couch like a fawn hiding from wolves. Wilma was born the year before the crops began to fail and the great walls of dust erupted from their fields and roared east, uprooting livelihoods faster than any stock market crash. He'd done his best to shield her from suffering, but for her it was just life. Not better than before because it was all she knew. Small portions and loose clothes that inflated like ship's sails when they caught the wind.

Daryl released his grip on the shotgun and propped it against his chair. His steps were like thunder, though he was not a large man. It was just so still, as if a giant kettle had been placed over their slice of Colorado. He crouched in front of his daughter and brushed the hair from her cheek.

"We don't need the stars, my love. I'd rather count your freckles," he said, tapping the bridge of her nose.

She smiled and squirmed away from him. Had the circumstances been different it would have been a joyous time, the family with full bellies, no worries about the wilted plants or bad eggs. No work to be done, soil to be tended.

"Mom?" Derek whispered.

The smile on her face was more genuine than any he recalled in recent times. It sparked a sprout of wrinkles around her eyes, pulled the skin taut over her cheekbones.

"Yes?"

Derek left his place by the fire and reached a handout. Darlene tried to take it. For a moment, she was confused, not horrified. Realization came quick, and her eyes reminded Derek of the cow when they took its dead calf away. As with the egg, as with Sam in the church, she was disappearing.

"Mama!" Wilma scrambled over the cushions.

Derek and Daryl wrapped their arms around her as if that could prevent what was coming.

Her chest rose and fell, heart humming against Derek's ear.

"It's okay. It's okay. It doesn't hurt. It doesn't hurt. Wherever I'm going, look for me when you get there. It's okay. It's okay," she said.

"I love you, Mama! Don't leave me!" Wilma squealed.

Derek sobbed quietly as there was less and less of her to hold.

The family, reduced by one member, met in an embrace. Wilma's entire small body shook, tears and snot flowing freely. A mixture of grief and fear, as the reality of her own vulnerability planted roots. In hours, minutes, or seconds she might begin to disappear.

WHUMP

Dust fell from the ceiling, and a book toppled off the mantle. It sounded like a bag of feed had been hurled at the house. Daryl looked to the window, eyes darting to the shotgun, but he did not leave his children.

"I'm s-scared, Daddy. I don't wanna disappear."

He could not tell her she wouldn't. He did not know if that was true. Any words he spoke might be his last, and he did not want them to be lies. Daryl balled his hands into fists. He could not beat this into submission. He could not kill it with his shotgun or burn it as with fields that failed to yield. He could only hold the girl and hope it would not be for the last time.

They cried until their bones ached, until the only respite was sleep. Derek and Wilma shared a bed for the first time in years as their father parked himself in a chair facing the front door, shotgun in hand. The porch floorboards squeaked and popped intermittently, the sound of failed attempts at stealth, of a creature navigating a new surface.

He found streaks on the living room window, slimy trails wider than his hand. But what created them hid in the deepening dark beneath a sky void of stars and a pinhole moon.

Maybe it would be better to disappear.

Daryl hid the window behind the curtain. This would not end well. The only question to be answered was when he would go, before or after his children. He propped the shotgun against the table, the plate of uneaten cookies at its center, and began to write.

Derek and Wilma,

He stared into the fire and waited for the words to come.

DEREK DREAMED, AGAIN, OF THE CARNIVAL. IT BEGAN pleasant, pulled from recent memories of flashing lights and popcorn, then shifted. The voices and laughter fell away, lights expiring like fireflies abandoning hope. He realized he was alone, pennies in one hand and the other no longer holding Wilma's. A shriek pulled Derek from sleep. His body stiffened. In the window. It was white as bone, head like a horse stripped of its skin. As its nostrils flared it blew mucus onto the window. Its tongue, the same pearly white, probed the window glass, twisting and turning. And then it was gone.

The sounds from outside were almost insect-like. Skittering noises mixed with chirps. Derek eased from beneath his sister's arm, one eye on the window as he padded out of the room. There was little light in the main body of the house, just a hint of orange from the few coals left in the fireplace.

"Dad?" Derek whispered.

He searched his parent's bedroom by feel, still calling for his father. He was not there. He was not in any of the rooms. There was a scrap of paper in the fireplace, its edges charred but some of the writing still legible.

We wait for dawn, we pray for light,
We are alone, and it is only ever night.

Derek found the shotgun on the floor in front of the locked front door of the house, where his father stood guard until...

The weapon still held a bit of his father's warmth. He claimed it, and his father's post, and parted the curtain.

Beyond the porch there was nothing but pitch black. No gray cornstalks. Nothing.

Derek unlocked the front door. He aimed the shotgun and stepped onto the porch. here was no difference in the world he saw with his eyes closed. He walked down the steps, and the sound of wood creaking caused a ripple effect in the insect noises both near and far. The hairs along his neck prickled, blood tingling in his fingertips.

The moon was all that remained in the night sky. It was a single point of light, a tiny, glowing grain of sand.

But he was not alone.

The clicks and chirps echoed over and around him. He recalled a school lesson about bats and how they navigated through the dark. He did not remember the term for it, but wondered if there were horse-headed creatures nearby who could see him just fine.

Inside, Derek added the last of the logs to the embers. He nudged Wilma awake and told her about their father. She wept, quietly, into his shoulder as he watched the window. When she was done they returned to the living room, moths to the flame.

WHUMP

The house shook from the impact. Insect noises followed, then a second WHUMP from their parent's bedroom.

"I'm scared, Derek," Wilma said.

"Me too."

As they sat, huddled together, shotgun nearby, Wilma began to hum.

"What is that?" Derek asked. "The song."

"Hm? Oh, I don't remember."

Derek remembered. It was the carnival music.

From his parent's bedroom a WHUMP was followed by the sound of glass splintering.

"Come on. I have an idea," Derek said.

They changed out of their pajamas in the darkness of their shared bedroom. Derek escorted his sister to the old Ford. There were whispers and wet clicks all around them.

"I'll be back. Two seconds."

He darted back inside the house, which was the only source of light now that the moon was gone, and emerged brandishing a flaming log. It swiveled back and forth at the end of the poker. He roared as he flung it into the cornfield, dry as autumn leaves. Thin white bodies with oversized heads fled the conflagration.

"Why did you…" Wilma began, but she was transfixed.

Derek thought for a moment, watching as the fire spread across the brittle grass of the front yard and licked the porch steps.

"For Dad. When I was little, before you were born, he loved the fields. Loved the work. But that was a long time ago."

They drove down the dirt path to town, darkness eating the waxy cones cast by the headlights. Wilma rambled about childish things, her mood shifting from happy to mournful. Near the edge of town Derek eased the car to a stop.

It stood in the road within a cloud of dust kicked up by the Ford, taller than a man though its back was hunched, as if accustomed to stooping in caverns with low ceilings. Its skin, now coated with Colorado dirt, was gray like the slugs Derek sometimes used as bait for fishing.

It turned its head to the side, showing a wide canal where ears might have been on a horse. Wilma dug her fingernails into Derek's forearm, and neither of them noticed. The creature swiveled its head back and forth, sending clicks and chirps at the car and into the darkness beyond. As Derek reached for the shotgun the beast lumbered off the road, its knuckles grazing the ground.

Wilma fell silent. She stared at the black outside the window, still gripping her brother's arm. At any moment he or she might disappear. If it was inevitable, he hoped to last just a little while longer.

He reached the carnival entrance and drove through it. Some attractions were already taken down, bundled up and loaded into truck beds. He rolled down his window. There was still a faint smell of popcorn and fried dough in the air. At last, the headlights illuminated the ride Derek hoped was still standing.

They stepped out of the car into the night. Derek left the Ford's lights on as he worked on the levers. There was a key in the generator, which sputtered to life when he turned it. The Ferris Wheel lit up, bulbs lining its borders. Wilma shielded her eyes, smiling and turning away.

"Come on," Derek said, taking her hand and leading her up the steps.

He escorted her to a gondola and closed the door.

"What about you?" she asked, gripping the car, not willing to sit.

Derek nodded to the panel with its various levers.

"Gotta get the thing going."

"Okay."

After a bit of trial-and-error, Derek sent the gondola to the top of the Ferris Wheel and halted it there. Then, he climbed the spokes and slid through a gap in the metal cage as Wilma scooted to make room.

"It's strange, isn't it?" he asked. "To see the sky like that."

She handed him a cookie.

"I wonder where we are now," she murmured.

The calliope music combined with the chug of the generator blocked the sound of insect noises. When Derek closed his eyes, it was easy to imagine he was back at the carnival and the world was right, that the past day or days had been a dream. He could almost hear the excited chatter of children, the carnival barkers lusting for the loose change in the pockets of rubes.

He hugged his little sister around her shoulders. The Ferris Wheel was her favorite. She couldn't handle the other rides yet, would always chicken out when she reached the front of the line. But that was okay. The Ferris Wheel was just fine with him.

Off in the distance there was an orange glow, the growing blaze he'd set minutes before. If he squinted, it almost looked like a sunrise.

THE RETURN OF THE CHAMPION

The ship had not responded in days, which stretched into a month and then years. It was like a decade-long funeral, a stream of casseroles in disposable pans, distant relatives and hangers-on hoping their loose affiliation might be captured by a local news camera. Flower deliveries appeared on her doorstep from time to time. Often, they were from her father-in-law, the card bearing either his name or a bit of broken English. For Miranda there was no cemetery, no headstone or urn. For Miranda there was just the night sky and its thoughtless, glimmering starlight.

They both understood the risk, that the journey eliminated the possibility of the couple being anything more than that. Under the best circumstances, she would be pushing fifty when he returned. Adoption was not off the table, but it was also rarely discussed. Not with the mission before him. Its demands upon his body and attention pared down their bond to its most basic form. Pecks on the cheek and an *I love you* hurled over the shoulder. Meals in the refrigerator with cooking instructions left on the kitchen island.

The Champion, with its new, untested and unproven technology, departed Earth bound for the far reaches of the solar system, the domain of gas giants. The scientific goal was to research the *anomaly* as it was dubbed, something between the orbits of Uranus and Neptune, which was not viewable from Earth, but its effects were detected. Whatever it was, it was big.

With that nebulous aim they began counting their lasts. The last dinner, the last love making, and finally, the last embrace in a room with his fellow astronauts and dozens of their family members and friends. Her group was comparatively small, their muted voices drowned in a sea of squeals and guffaws. Questions gnawed at her, questions she should have asked months ago or made peace with not knowing. Why not send a probe? Why dispatch a crew on the most dangerous voyage in mankind's history for *research*?

She spotted her husband, Capt. Michael Torres, at a dinner party a few weeks prior to launch. He was the focal point of a small collection of mousy men swimming in ill-fitting suits. Michael gesticulated wildly, his unrestrained smile indicative of both excitement and fear. As Miranda neared, one of the pale mouse-men nodded in her direction, the mood of the conversation shifting, eyes directed at glasses of wine yet to be sampled.

"Just sports, honey," he told her, his smile within normal limits.

She was an artist, a poet and a writer, inspiration culled from observation. She understood there were specific terms her husband used to describe the anomaly when not in public, and the generalized nature of the voyage appeared to be a ruse. There were words he spoke when he thought she was out of earshot and an intensifying habit of looking not into her eyes but above her head, as if hoping to glimpse something still to come.

A born-again spinster, Miranda watched the night sky as if the stars would assemble themselves and spell out the answer to her question. *What happened to the Champion?*

The answer came eleven years after Capt. Torres and the crew scaled the platform to blow kisses to their loved ones. Almost exactly two years after mission day one the Champion stopped communicating. A rescue effort was discussed but never executed. In the time it would take to dispatch a new crew the Champion would be one hundred million miles further away, and only discoverable assuming it maintained its trajectory.

"Hello?" Miranda said, voice groggy with sleep.

"Mrs. Torres?"

"Yes, who is this?"

"It's Jack, from Houston. We've spoken once or twice before. There's no delicate way to say this, no way that won't make you think this is a prank call. But Mrs. Torres, they're back. They're on the way back. The crew. Your husband. We got the signal this morning. It was static at first, but we fixed it."

"You-what? Is this a joke?" Miranda said, hand pressed to her chest as if her heart might spring free of it.

"No, ma'am, and I apologize for the early morning call. You're likely going to be of public interest again, and I wanted you to have ample time to prepare."

"Where are they?"

"Well, if you had a model of the solar system, they would have passed Mars a month or so ago. We, the Earth I mean, are actually on opposite-"

"How long?"

"About a week. Give that a day or so as a buffer. But as of now about a week."

"You heard his voice?"

"Michael? Yes, we heard his voice. It'll be on the news in the morning. I'd play it for you now, but they're still cleaning it up."

"Are you able to send a message from me?"

She sensed his hesitation, a vague image of a man wearing a short sleeve shirt with a tie, scratching the back of his neck.

"I might. Might be able to send something. It's pretty busy in here as you can imagine."

"If you can, just tell him I hope he saved it for me. He'll understand."

"Will do, ma'am," he said, and hung up before she could ask another question.

THE ENTIRE WORLD WATCHED, IF NOT IN UNITY, THEN AT least curiosity. The lost crew, blazing through the atmosphere, back from the dead. Five-hundred million new souls joined humanity in the time since the Champion first departed. Wars were fought. Markets rose and tumbled. The world watched, not predicting tragedy but aware it was a possibility. Miranda watched, too, her blood feeling carbonated in her veins, the ship closer than it had been in a decade but the moment until its landing feeling limitless. She imagined herself trapped there forever, eyes fixed to the same screen with a never-ending loop of the Champion on fire.

A smattering of applause from family members of the crew. Miranda shook her head, the daydream evaporating. The Champion was safe.

He emerged and at once shielded his face from the sun. Just a glimpse, less than a second but she knew it was him. Miranda smoothed the skirt of her dress and checked her pocket mirror one last time. Would he recognize her? Her crimson hair streaked here and there with white? The thin lines carved into her forehead and sprouting from the corners of her eyes? She considered dyeing it. Considered fillers or a non-invasive lift. But this was her, for better or worse, and the last thing she wanted to do upon reuniting with her husband was wear a mask.

The other family members milled about in the waiting room, spouses and children, grandchildren named in honor of once-fallen heroes. Michael's mother passed away three years prior, not for a moment wavering in her belief her son would return. She died with his name on her lips, her syrupy eyes gazing through the hospital ceiling to the stars beyond. His father sat in the far corner, hair mostly silver, face browned by the sun, staring at a picture of his dead wife. Though language was always a barrier between them, Miranda shared his spirit, quiet but unconquerable. She crossed the room to place a hand on his shoulder.

They exchanged more glances than words. An hour as long as the Universe passed before a dainty man in a polo shirt entered the room.

"Thank you for your patience. We understand how eager you are to reconnect with your loved ones. As you can imagine, we have much to discuss with them. We will need them back in just a few minutes, but for now, ladies and gentlemen, your heroes have returned."

One by one they filed through the door clad in sweatpants and gray t-shirts, some with hair still damp from the shower. There were gasps and cheers, walks turning to sprints. Michael was the last to pass through the door. She kicked off her high heels rushing to greet him, shrinking by three inches, losing sight of him for a moment. Not all at once, but little by little she released a decade of anxiety, the muscles of her neck like thawing icicles.

His arms remained slack at his sides, his body twisted slightly away from her. He did not adjust to welcome her, only tilted his head with no expression on his face.

"Miranda?" he said, tone hovering between a statement and a question.

"Yes?" she retreated half a step to look at him.

Tears welled and she fought the urge to turn and run in the other direction, to keep running toward the strange comfort of the new life she created. He looked the same as the day he left, not a day older. She wilted under his gaze, cursing herself for not dyeing her hair to its former red. As soon as it left her the anxiety returned, snaking through her body and settling in her chest. How could it be the same? Ten years, billions of miles between them.

Michael watched the crew members interact with their families with a detached sort of interest, like a zookeeper passing the lion exhibit for the thousandth time. He returned his attention to his wife, then staring at the lacquer of her toenails.

"I'm home," he said, and wrapped his arms around her.

A minute later, his father approached, smiling in defiance of his watery eyes. In his hand, roughened from years in the field, he held the picture of Michael's mother.

"Michael?" the old man said.

Miranda moved aside and made space for him.

He was much shorter than his son, even with the added inches from his cowboy boots. They hugged and exchanged a few words in Spanish. He passed the photo to his son and nodded as Michael spoke in a soft voice.

Miranda had a thousand questions and a thousand more things to tell him, but the man in the polo shirt ended the reunion, with his sincere apologies.

SHE STALKED THE HOUSE LIKE A LISTLESS SPECTER, FLIPPING pillows and straightening pictures that had been through the process a half hour before. At midnight, still in her dress, she sat on the couch and turned the television on. His face was on every channel, the images of the crew departing the Champion. A press conference was held a couple of hours previous, but the astronauts fielded no questions.

He looked…sad.

Maybe not sad, but not happy either. Nor was he between the two emotions. His gaze swam around the room, never settling, unaware the majority of the questions were directed at him.

He was back, though. It was so far from plausible she wondered if the whole last week had been a fever dream. Perhaps she was in a hospital bed and the Champion was still lost. It happened too quickly. A month ago, her husband was the answer to a question on Jeopardy. Now he was back.

But where had he been?

She paused the television and studied his face. He was composed but not relaxed, flinching at the occasional camera flashes. Nostrils flaring when he spoke. Others would not have noticed it, but she did. She always noticed things like that.

She fell asleep without having realized it and dreamed of her husband. She dreamed of him often, in the beginning. Later, he became a sort of cryptid in her visions. She would hear him mashing avocados in the kitchen and follow the sound, hopeful, but he was never there. The evidence of him faded into the background, a pair of shoes in the hall, a wristwatch beside the shower.

When she woke and saw him standing, nude, in the living room she screamed.

"Are you coming to bed?" he asked.

"Is this a dream?"

He looked at the pictures on the wall behind her. Pictures of their wedding day and honeymoon. One picture of him waving to her from the platform the day the Champion launched into space.

"No, I am here," he said.

He offered his hand, and she took it, trailing slightly behind him as they walked to the master bedroom.

"How did you get home?" she asked.

"They drove me. Sorry I didn't wake you at first. You looked so peaceful sleeping, and they did not give us much time to shower."

"It's okay. I'm just glad you're back."

He walked around the bed to the left side, her side. He never slept on that side of the bed. But that was before. Did it matter? Nights when the longing turned to desperation, she wriggled free of the comforter to smell his unwashed pillowcase, which no longer bore his essence, and no longer matched the rest of the bedding. She slept where he once did and sometimes dreamed of she would wake to his gentle nudge, telling her she was on the wrong side of the bed.

Miranda fumbled with the zipper and glanced at Michael to see if he noticed. He hadn't. He stared at the picture on her nightstand, perhaps recognizing her things there. If so, he took no action. She slinked out of the dress and draped it over a chair then held her hands across her body, which was softer in the middle than he would have remembered. He had moved on from the nightstand and stood at the sliding glass door leading to the deck, hands on his hips and head tilted toward the stars. There was a tension in his posture, from fear or longing she could only guess. She slid between the sheets, grateful for the distraction.

When he joined her in bed and the lamps were turned off, her questions felt weightless. She reached for his hand and found it. For a long time, she said nothing, only listened to the melody of their breaths. How strange and wonderful it was, her center of gravity returned. Would they settle into a new orbit? Miranda drifted between waking and sleep, the union of their hands interrupted by dream-inspired twitches.

Finally, just before sunrise, she whispered, "Michael, what happened to you?"

He did not respond at once. He did not respond at all. She examined his face in the pale morning light, the smudged lines of his closed eyes. She listened to his breath, watched the rise and fall of his back.

She knew he was not asleep.

MICHAEL WAS GONE MORE THAN HE WAS AT HOME. TESTS, interviews, and more tests. At home the couple functioned as roommates, the right words said with little action to confirm them.

I love you! Shouted from across the room. Kisses as an obligation.

Miranda began to disrobe in private and shower with the bathroom door closed. The life they settled into was similar to their lives leading up to his departure, a mockery of the future they imagined for themselves as young lovers. She had so many questions. She had so many things to tell him. Though they had a lifetime ahead of them, somehow that brought no comfort. Michael was distracted, lost, his attention focused beyond her reach among the stars.

She noticed it during the press conference, but it was easy to dismiss considering all they'd been through. Her husband was uncomfortable, revealed in small ways. He tugged at the collar of his shirts. He pushed food around his plate, painting landscapes with sauces, but seldom ate.

"Miss your space food?" she asked him one evening.

She had prepared spaghetti, her mother's recipe. It was his favorite dish, though that fact had not passed between them. Miranda flitted between the dining room table and the kitchen, piling garlic bread into a towel-lined basket, fetching a block of parmesan and a grater. She mentioned that he was usually helping himself to seconds before she even sat down.

"That's right," he said, and smiled, the unblemished fork in hand.

Miranda left to retrieve a bottle of wine.

"Are they almost done with you?" she called from the kitchen.

"I am not sure. They haven't been satisfied with the answers we have given."

"About the...anomaly?"

"About all of it."

She returned moments later to find Michael wiping his lips on a napkin.

"Just like I remember it," he said.

Their conversation had not found a natural rhythm in the weeks since he returned. She had many questions, but Michael had no answers. For him, the previous decade had been like a dreamless slumber. Perhaps that explained the difference in their disposition, his comparative aloofness against her desperation to make up for lost time. She felt every minute of his absence and he slept through it.

Michael took a call and Miranda finished the meal in silence. She cleared the table and stood over the trash can ready to scrape the stray strands she no longer had an appetite for. Instead, she placed the plate on the kitchen island and pinched a corner of Michael's napkin. There were several of them. As she tugged it unraveled spilling its spaghetti guts. He had not eaten a bite. It was all hidden in the napkins. Miranda screamed.

She stomped through the house and found him outside on the deck, neck craned toward the stars. He turned as the door opened and smiled when he saw her.

"What happened to you!?"

She wiped her nose with the back of her hand.

His posture was not defensive. He hooked his thumbs through the belt loops of his pants. He had to know this was coming, but still, he could not say the words she needed. In his silence, she sensed the forging of a new reality, another lie glimmering with a fresh coat of varnish.

"What happened to you up there?" she said, lips rippling and teeth clenched.

Michael followed her gaze back to the stars and ran his fingers through his ebon hair.

"It became home. It began to feel like home. The darkness. The void. We got so far away I didn't know where Earth was. It was just us and the darkness."

It didn't feel like a lie. Nor did it reveal some new truth. She stepped out of the house, crossed the creaking wood of the deck and stood in his gauzy shadow. Frogs squelched in hidden pools as birds of prey stretched their wings in high perches. It was familiar. The sounds of the night coming alive. For years she stood in that same place, shivering or sweating, wondering if her share of the night sky included him.

"That's not good enough. What happened to you? Where did you go for almost ten years? How did you survive? What did you see?" she demanded.

He nodded, accepting each question and the blame of not having told her before. He bridged the distance between them by taking her hands.

"I don't know if you will like my answer."

His tone was flat, a fact simply stated.

"You have to tell me something. We gave up our chance to be a family for this."

He wiped a tear from her cheek.

"The answer is, I do not know. It was normal. The mission was on track. Then darkness. Real darkness. My next memory is of finding myself in command of the ship, flying past Mars."

"You don't know?"

He shook his head.

"What about before? What happened just before?"

He shook his head again.

"There wasn't a before. Everything was normal, as I said. In my mind I blinked, and now I am here, with you, confused and learning how to be me."

It was not the explanation she needed, but Miranda was beginning to accept it might not exist.

"Did you save it for me?"

He smiled, "Save what?"

Her heart sank at the confidence behind his confusion.

"You said you would save me a jarful of stardust. It was something you told me to help ease my mind. Just a silly thing."

MIRANDA THOUGHT THEY MIGHT MAKE LOVE FOR THE FIRST time since Michael returned. His touch, a hand on her hip or squeeze of her arm was still tentative, but she sensed the need behind it. As she bathed, he took a phone call and spent the next hour offering one-word responses while pacing through the house.

It was progress, though, the tension between them finally acknowledged. There was a playfulness in his smile as he passed her, cell phone pressed to one ear. Their conversation on the deck was the closest to vulnerable he'd come. And she didn't need him to explain the miracle of his return. Leave it to the folks in Houston to put the pieces together.

Her cell phone chimed as she exited the bath. It was a number only friends and family knew, and so she was surprised to discover the sender was neither.

Miranda this is Jack from Houston. I shouldn't be telling you this but something is wrong. They're tight-lipped about it here but

I'm worried. One of the Russian cosmonauts died yesterday morning. Not public info. But that's not the real story. During the autopsy they found things were…off. He didn't have fillings. In his dental exam 11 years ago he had 7. I don't know what it means. There's a lot happening here people aren't talking about. Stay safe and delete this message.

"Who was it?" Michael asked, startling a breath from her.

She tightened her robe and smiled, "Oh, my mom. She wants to know when we're going to visit."

Michael smiled and turned his attention to his phone again, "You decide."

She lay in bed for an hour, listening to his passage through the house. More questions and one-word answers.

There's a lot happening here people aren't talking about.

She hadn't asked him about the spaghetti. That was the final straw for her, and she hadn't asked about it. What did it mean? Did it mean anything at all? And what did a cosmonaut's dental history have to do with anything?

She resisted the urge to reply to Jack but checked her phone every minute for an hour. Without planning to, she fell asleep with the phone on her chest.

In her dream she woke to an empty bed. It was dark in the room, both bedside lamps extinguished. She first looked to the window, where she discovered him some nights, gazing at the stars. He must have had the same questions as her. Almost twenty percent of his life passed in an instant.

He was not at the window, and his side of the bed was cool. Beneath the bedroom door there were no lights, nothing to indicate he was elsewhere within the house. She glided to the window and stood where he so often did. She parted the curtains and saw moonlight reflected off the deck, so bright she had to squint. There was something else in the dark, in the yard near the line of trees. A dog? No. It was a person.

It was Michael.

Miranda cupped her hands around her face and pressed her nose to the glass. He was shirtless and hunched over, limbs in frantic motion. She placed knuckles on the glass and nearly tapped, but instead waited.

What are you doing?

As if in answer to her question he whipped his head around. Soil spilled from his mouth onto his naked chest. Miranda stumbled backwards, confused and disgusted. He licked a hillock of sparkling earth from his palm, then walked toward the deck, his belly like a small mountain.

She woke with a jolt and gasped to find his face inches from hers. He brushed a wisp of hair from her cheek and smiled. No soil on his teeth, no mania in his eyes.

"Is it too late?"

Her pounding hear steadied.

"Too late?"

"For a family?"

It was such a shocking question she could only blink in response.

"What?"

"Physically. Are you still able?"

His hand settled on her belly. His touch was warm, and her skin tingled beneath it.

"I-I *am* getting hot flashes and my cycle is erratic…"

"But…"

"I don't know. Even if I was, we haven't talked about it."

His hand inched south, and her blood followed. She leaned into his touch. Eleven years. It had been eleven years. Eleven years of longing, of scrutinizing every star hoping it was him.

It wasn't like before. His kisses were reluctant and clumsy, as if he was a teenager again. He felt different, as well, fixated on the visceral aspect of their coupling rather than her need for connection. But, she thought, it had been eleven years for him, too. As was so often true in their relationship, her pleasure would come later.

He finished, and she was not satisfied, but there was always tomorrow. She sat up, intending to go to the bathroom to clean herself, but he placed a hand on her shoulder.

"It might be our only chance," he said.

It was true, and she did not know what her preference was regarding the implication, but she lay down until sleep claimed her.

His cell rang, yanking her out of a dreamless slumber. He took the phone out of the bedroom before answering it.

It was after 3 AM. Miranda hobbled to the toilet, legs unaccustomed to the strain of bearing his weight. Her cell phone chimed, and she waddled back to the bedroom to retrieve it.

It was a video message from Jack.

It took her a few moments to orient herself to the small image on the screen. Jack appeared to have filmed a monitor in the control room. She squinted at it and turned the volume up. The picture was fuzzy, interrupted by static, and the audio was difficult to discern.

"…Torres of the Champion. I repeat…of the Champion…headed back to Earth. They are not us! For… love of God…not us!"

It was Michael, a version of him. Sallow cheeks and a patchy beard sprinkled with gray. He was thin and haggard, but it was Michael.

A text followed the video.

Get out of there!

She felt a trickle course down her inner-thigh and touched it with her fingertips. It was gritty, like aloe mixed with sand, and dark gray in color. It reminded her of the slugs that polluted their deck after a thunderstorm.

He stood in the doorway and looked at her with Michael's eyes.

"What are you?" she whispered, pressing her back against the wall.

He did not answer but looked to the window, and the night beyond. Michael was out there somewhere. Michael was coming home.

The man in the doorway tossed the cell phone onto the floor. He turned off the light and stepped into the room.

"Wh-what do you want from me?"

He stopped, confusion rippling across his face, "You wanted the stars, Miranda. I have seen them."

"No I-"

"I will take you there, and far beyond."

Miranda eyed the door to the deck. If she reached it before he reached her, then what?

"You worry about your age. I have heard every thought, every question you did not speak. I am sorry for the deception, though that is a word for a feeling I have never known."

"What...what are you?"

Michael, or whatever was pretending to be him, began to unbutton his shirt.

"There are no words in your language to explain it."

Miranda's cell phone rang. She did not answer it. Help would not come quick enough, she knew.

He displayed two fingers, turned them into hooks.

"But I can show you."

His fingers disappeared within his bellybutton. He pulled, the skin stretching beyond what should have been the limits of the flesh. Moonlight oozed through the slats of the blinds, its silver-blue light flaring over his midsection, over the expanding hole.

Miranda's vision narrowed, the walls closing in. A great tide of nothingness washed over her, filling her ears. Her extremities felt disconnected from her; the fingers might as well have been balloons. She felt only the cooling residue on her inner thigh and wondered what it meant for her.

It was funny, though. The form emerging from her husband's skin, flaring here and there where the moonlight touched it, did remind her of stardust.

FAMILY ANNIHILATOR

There's a tooth in my knuckle, Nancy's I think, don't remember hitting either kid in the face. She turned her head at just the right moment so that the blow destined to knock her out instead rearranged the architecture of her mouth. The second blow did it, but there was that moment of awkward eye contact I'll probably think about the rest of the week.

I have never killed a person. I would pass a lie detector test corroborating the same. Yes, many people have died as a direct result of my actions, but I have no blood on my hands, no blood on my gloves either. That is admittedly difficult to claim with Nancy's tooth burrowed into my knuckle. When she dies, though, it will not be my finger on the trigger, my hand grasping the knife.

It is the first week of summer. Doug left for work at 6:30 AM as he always does. The kids and Nancy were at home, sleeping in. He is not expected at work until 8:00 AM, but Doug leaves early to beat the traffic, he says. He actually leaves early to jack off in the office parking lot. He keeps baby wipes in the car solely for this purpose.

Doug and Nancy stay together for the kids. No, I don't sneak into their home to read Nancy's diary. I haven't created an online alter ego to catfish them. It's obvious to anyone paying attention, which most people don't do.

Nancy has a crush on the Amazon guy. It's both pathetic and fascinating watching her perform. Heels and denim skirts she bought at Target fifteen years ago, a blouse with a strategic button undone. Last week, she answered the door in a towel, made a big show of how embarrassed she was. I imagine she was sitting in that towel all day, one eye on the door, pretending there was some other reason she had not dressed by one o'clock. She probably knew this would not be possible when the kids were home for summer. I bet she thought about it for weeks. It may be the only thing keeping her going.

Doug does not know this version of Nancy. He knows sweatpants with the tired elastic band, t-shirts from a 5K run neither would attempt today. He knows a Nancy not missing an incisor.

Doug mostly jacks off in the car.

We are in Doug's "man cave" right now. Nancy and the kids are incapacitated, though the teenage son keeps waking up. I keep putting him back to sleep. I would be concerned at the number of concussions he sustained in such a short period of time if not for the reality of his impending death. I think the daughter, Kaylee, is pretending to be unconscious, which is okay. Pretending is just as good as being for my purpose.

I can feel her eyes on my back as I put Kristopher (yes, with a K) to sleep for a few more minutes.

As I mentioned, I have never killed anyone. I do, however, put things into place that make death almost inevitable. ("Almost" is doing *a lot* of work in that sentence) Think of it like toppling dominoes. I give the first domino a nudge. Is it my fault if at the end of the column there is a severed head, or an uncorked jugular? (That's a messy description, but I like the visual) My only rule is I do not bring anything into the house except my wits. Why? If I wanted to kill people, I could just do it. It isn't terribly challenging or interesting. It isn't the killing I care about. It is everything leading up to it. It is everything after.

Caught in a moment of reverie. I apologize. I pluck Nancy's tooth from my knuckle and drop it into my fannypack. I wish there was another word for fannypack. It really takes the legs out of what I am trying to achieve here. During my early forays I learned there would be items (evidence) necessary to remove from the scene. Feels a bit ridiculous carrying a plastic baggie in my pocket and the fannypack also holds my Pop-Tarts. I'm no good without a snack.

Tooth secured in the front, zippered pocket, I take stock of my surroundings. Just as I wish there was a better name for fannypack, I wish there was a worse descriptor for "man cave". There is an old, big screen television facing a burgundy, pleather couch leaking stuffing. The glass coffee table has cum stains on it, I think. In addition to balled tissues there is an obelisk on the table, a team award from work Doug claimed for himself. Posters of athletes who retired two Presidents ago leer from the walls.

The furniture found a second, sadder life after its service in the family living room, I guess. None of this is who Doug *is*. It's not even who he wishes to be. It's who he thinks others wish him to be. Pair this with Nancy's cavorting and I conclude they are both better off dead. If they live average lives Doug will be jacking off in the office parking lot for twenty-five more years. Nancy will probably end up on the sex offender roster.

The kids? Well, it wouldn't be a family annihilation without the kids.

There are ropes, cinderblocks, a few random knives, an open safe that probably has a handgun in it. And so much duct tape. It should be enough.

I think Doug is slowly moving from the master bedroom to this unfortunate cave. There is a little refrigerator next to the couch, a mobile clothes rack with half of Doug's work wardrobe. The robe draped over the couch and slippers beneath it suggest he either completes his morning routine in this room or sleeps here now. I rifle through his collection of ties in a set of plastic drawers and select three.

"I knew you were faking," I whisper in Kaylee's ear. She recoiled at my approach, turned her face away as I kneeled beside her. I blind her with a tie, wave my hand in front of her face to be sure. Tape across the mouth. Good to go.

Kristopher has learned his lesson. As I approach, he begins to snore. Not that it matters now, but it looks like there is a jellyfish beneath his scalp, a palm-sized contusion that wiggles as he breathes. Couple more blows and I might have done the thing I said I never do.

"Why are you doing this?" Nancy asks, blood spilling out her mouth.

Yep, that was *her* tooth.

"Doing what?"

She scoffs, spits a little blood on her sweatpants (no Amazon delivery today I guess).

"Look, sorry about the tooth. That's really not the point of this."

"What *is* the point? Are you going to rape me?"

"With that missing tooth? Are you serious?"

She begins to cry. I forget what it's like to be on the other side. Most of my jokes bomb, but every now and then I'll get a chuckle.

"Hey, it's not about the tooth. I wouldn't have before the tooth thing. Look up."

She does and I place tape across her mouth, brushing aside a few strands of her honey-blonde hair so they are not trapped beneath it. I blind her with a tie.

"You can breathe okay?"

She nods her head.

"Good. Again, sorry about the tooth."

There is no standard reaction to having your home invaded. Fight or flight leaves out the most common response, which is to freeze. Not like a statue. They aren't hoping to blend into the wallpaper, afraid any movement will catch my eye. They're not frozen solid. More like slush. As the waves of adrenaline settle into the marrow exhaustion takes hold.

Yes, Nancy feared for her life and for the lives of her children. That didn't stop her from falling asleep a minute after I taped her mouth shut.

If I know Doug, the video cassettes labeled "College Game '16" or "Jeopardy and WoF" are actually porn. I don't play them. I do turn on the television and increase the volume so my actions within the room are obscured.

Why are you doing this?

It's the question they always ask, and one that I will never understand.

What can I do to not be murdered?

That's a better question, although most people fool themselves about that eventuality. They think, or hope, they are being robbed. Nancy thinks I'm in it for the sex. If I wanted that from her I could have bought an Amazon uniform.

I am afraid to answer the question of why. If I had the answer I might not feel the need to do this.

Kristopher struggles against the restraints. Many teenage boys use this moment to become men. They attempt to, at least. He is bound to a support pillar near the small window that glimpses the backyard. His mother and sister are bound to support pillars near me, and the fourth pillar is unoccupied save for an electronic dartboard hung from a nail.

There are a few exposed beams crossing the width of the man cave. I see potential in this space, room to unshackle my imagination. Ropes and knives, tape and ceiling beams. The television is probably heavy enough to kill Kaylee, but that uncertainty feels like a mistake waiting to happen. I'd probably have to lift the television to check, and if she survived it could get messy. I hate do-overs.

Still, I like the elements in this room. It's small but not claustrophobic. No danger of stepping on Nancy while I'm working on Kristopher.

I scale the stairs halfway, imagining how Doug will see the room in a few hours. There will be less natural light then, but enough for him to understand something is wrong. He'll walk through the house first, calling for Nancy and the kids. Her car is in the driveway, keys hanging on the same hook as her purse. He'll call her cell and find it upstairs.

Eventually, he'll make his way to the man cave, maybe hoping he'll have time to watch "College Game '16" before the family returns. There is no overhead light, just a floor lamp. He'll stop where I am standing right now, trying to make sense of the strange shadows in this room he knows so well. Maybe the smell will hit him then, the copper mixed with the saltwater reek of his night sweat soaked into the stuffing of the couch.

Depending on how the scene plays out, he may have to step over a body to reach the floor lamp. From there, my mind loses track of the possibilities. He will try to save them, learning one-by-one they cannot be saved. He will press his shaking fingers into the hollows of cooling necks, searching for a pulse.

I am counting on it, Doug.

Don't let me down.

I AM THANKFUL DOUG BUYS DUCT TAPE FROM COSTCO. I finish setting things up with two rolls to spare. Sometimes I find only half a roll. Maybe I am too dependent on it. What if the next house has no duct tape?

Kristopher flinches when the rope contacts his skin. I peel the tape from his mouth, taking the pale, pathetic beginnings of his first mustache with it.

"Hey, uh, sorry about the mustache," I whisper, and he cringes as my breath tickles the fine hair of his ear. "Why, um, why do you spell it with a K?"

He cocks his head.

"Your name," I clarify. "Why Kristopher with a K? Is it like a family thing, or…"

"I-it was Mom's idea."

Doesn't really answer my question, but I'll move on from it. I tape his mouth shut.

He squirms as I tighten the rope. Tears leak from under the tie.

"Gonna need you to stand, Kristopher with a K."

He does.

"Gonna need you to stand on this," I say nudging the stool so that it contacts his knee.

He shakes his head.

"I'll cut your dick off."

He stands on the stool, bound hands held in front of him for balance.

I walk the rope across the room and kneel beside Nancy. She alternates between sleeping and crying. I hope

I judged her love for her children correctly. These next ten minutes depend on it.

"Hey," I whisper, peeling the tape from her mouth. "You're not a K and Doug's not a K. Why give your kids K names?"

Nancy spits. It lands on her daughter.

"Okay, jeez."

I tape her mouth again and loop the rope around her waist. I give it a little tug and Kristopher flinches across the room. Perfect.

Kaylee looks like a half-aborted attempt at a robot mummy. The tape covers her legs from the knees down, masks her arms from the elbows up. She fell asleep, taped to the board previously used to stabilize a broken foot of the couch.

"Up up," I whisper in her ear. "Like a plank. You know what that is?"

She pushes herself into a plank position. The board is trapped within a prison of cinderblocks and duct tape. She can move it a few inches toward her stomach but not left, right, or above the level of her clavicle. I tap the broken off butcher's knife blade into the slot I carved for it. The tip of the blade is about two inches from her sternum.

"Okay, you gotta stay that way. There's a knife under you now and-" my words are interrupted by her scream. As she made no sounds to that point, I had no cause to silence her. "I should have said not to scream first."

Nancy is upset. She thrashes her head, stretches her jaw attempting to loosen the tape.

"Hold still," I say, scraping a corner of tape free of her cheek before ripping it off.

"What's going on?!" Nancy shouts, attempting to stand without the use of her duct-taped hands. She scoots forward a few inches, pulling the rope looped around her waist taut. Kristopher teeters on the stool, tries to yell but the effort dies in the glue binding the tape to his face.

I help Nancy to her feet and pull the tie free from her eyes. They balloon like an animated wolf in an old Tex Avery cartoon. They land on me for a second.

It's the strangest thing, and it happens every time. *I* am the person who hammered the blade into the board beneath her daughter's chest. *I* am the person who gave Nancy an unplanned tooth extraction. There is no anger in her gaze, something closer to somber confusion.

Now, I fade into the background. Everything is up to Nancy and the kids.

Nancy fights against the rope without realizing the source of the resistance. She stretches her duct tape mittens toward her daughter, screaming for her to not move. Her voice is like an uncomfortable violin note, wavering and thin. Kaylee is screaming as well, the cacophony of their combined terror obscures the choked snorts from Kristopher, standing on tip-toe as the rope looped over the ceiling beam and wrapped around Nancy's waist constricts his throat.

"It's right below you, honey! Don't drop!" Nancy yells.

She plants her dominant leg and pushes, a surge of parental adrenaline propelling her forward another six inches. Kristopher pirouettes for a second and then dangles, rope cutting off blood and oxygen. Nancy slides backwards, but her focus is three feet in front of her. She does not turn and instead uses the pillar to push herself toward her daughter.

Within five seconds, Kristopher's face is the color of a tomato forgotten in the back of the pantry, red mixing with eggplant purple. His legs kick, causing him to sway. Nancy feels the tug of his body, but it does not penetrate. Her focus is singular, the girl hovering inches above a blade aimed right at her heart. Nancy digs her heels in, pushes harder. Kristopher kicks his legs, reclaiming Nancy's hard-fought inches.

The first domino has been nudged. Everything that happens now is inevitable.

"Baby, you're dipping! You have to stay strong, honey! I'm trying to reach you!"

And if she does, what then? What is she going to do with her duct tape mittens? Maybe she could flip Kaylee on her back without wrenching her knees out their sockets. (I used *a lot* of tape) Maybe she can will her arms to grow two feet longer and swat the blade aside.

Kaylee dips a couple of inches, just enough to touch the tip of the knife. She screams again, a tiny spot of red blossoming on her shirt.

"You can do anything, baby. You can stay like that for an hour if you need!"

(I disagree!)

Kristopher is running in slow motion, now. The last ten yards of a marathon. Blood flows freely from both nostrils.

"I'm almost there!"

(She is no closer than she was fifteen seconds ago)

Nancy, just pretend it's the Amazon guy! I laugh and cover my mouth. Nancy does not hear. When she is not vomiting false hope for her daughter she is grunting, fighting against the weight of her son, whose legs are now limp.

TUNK

TUNK

The crown of Kristopher's head rams into the beam. Nancy looks at her feet as if they are to blame for her inability to reach her daughter.

"I can't Mom!" Kaylee sobs.

"Yes you can! You can do anything, baby. Just…send your mind somewhere else."

Nancy grunts these last words and rams her son's head into the beam hard enough for the wood to thrum.

"Think of Christmas! J-just think tomorrow is Christmas," Nancy says.

The effort to speak these words syphons precious oxygen from her lungs. She cannot be still. Her feet slide backwards the moment she relaxes, and she loses half a foot. She swallows, sweat shining on her forehead. The resignation etched into her face softens into something new.

Recognition.

She looks at her mittens, lifts her arms to judge how much territory remains between herself and Kaylee.

"Mom! I can't!"

"Y-you have to, sweetheart. You have to."

Kaylee dips again, tries to relax her lower torso without contacting the blade and fails. More blood, the stain spreads like a red Rorschach.

Nancy has no plan. Her eyes follow phantom steps across the carpet. We briefly make eye contact, and I am again reminded of the tooth incident from an hour ago. She does not see me for what I am, the man who put these dominoes into place. She sees me as her last hope, her potential savior.

As she comes to terms with the inevitable in front of her, it has already taken place behind. Kristopher is dead. There may be a few sparks going off upstairs, a final spasm of a heart which has only known one function its entire existence. But he is dead, the cord stretching between his body and his mother no longer sustaining life but ending it.

"Mom!"

"I'm almost there, sweetheart."

This is still not true, but what else can she say? She tries. She stretches a leg out instead of an arm but is only able to hold the position for a second, the tip of her toe close enough to Kaylee's head to flutter her hair.

"Mom?"

Nancy, careens backward, bracing herself against the pillar just before Kristopher touches the floor.

"Mom?"

"I'm sorry," Nancy whispers.

She will have to make a choice. To watch or to turn away. Tears spill, but she quiets the welling sobs.

"Mom? I…it hurts. It hurts so much I can't…"

"I-I know, sweetheart."

Each time Kaylee dips the knife goes a little deeper. Maybe she's getting used to the pain, which might be less than the burn in her muscles elsewhere.

"Can't you do something?" Kaylee says.

"I...I..."

The knife breaks through the tissue, contacts the sternum.

"Aaahhh!!" Kaylee wails, the pitch rising in octave as it escapes her.

"I'm sorry!" Nancy shouts.

"Mom, you have to do something!"

Nancy looks at her mittens, looks at the floor. Suddenly, she stands. Oh, this is interesting. She wriggles a foot free of its slipper. It dangles from her big toe. Kaylee's whole body is beginning to shake, rippling from neck to calves.

"I-I'm gonna try something," Nancy says.

She closes one eye as if aiming and flings the slipper toward the blade. It taps Kaylee on the head and falls to the floor.

"What was that?!"

"I'm trying to cover the knife. Y-you might be able to put some weight on it and then shift it."

If she does that I'm just going to reset the dominoes, but Nancy has forgotten about me.

"Okay, Mom."

Nancy dangles her other slipper, closes one eye and flings.

She almost did it.

The heel of the shoe glances off the blade. Had it been half an inch higher, my dinner plans would have been delayed by fifteen minutes.

"Did it work?" Kaylee asks.

Nancy sobs, turns away. Her hands cover her face.

"It-it's okay Mom. I love you."

"I'm sorry."

"Is it going to hurt?"

Nancy faces her daughter again.

"Probably at first. It'll go quick, though."

She dips again, knife scoring bone.

"Kristopher, I love you, too," Kaylee says.

Nancy blinks a few times, looks to the rope around her waist. An idea forms, but it's like a dark shape in the water, unknowable from the surface.

"I'm sorry, Mom. I'm sorry I couldn't hold out longer. I'm gonna-"

It is inadvertent. She falls on the blade, a sound like a cat running over hot coals escaping her lips.

"Kaylee!"

Nancy finds a second wind (probably fifth if I am being literal) and thrusts her mittens at her daughter, bare heels desperate for purchase. Animal noises spill from her mouth as bloody butterfly wings spread beneath her daughter's now still body.

After twenty seconds of this, she collapses, allows the rope to pull her backwards.

If I am going to continue with the dominoes analogy, now we're approaching the tricky part, rounding a corner or scaling a stack of books. This is where it can all go wrong.

Nancy weeps, her hair a stringy curtain blocking her face from view. Kaylee's blood encroaches upon her space, enters her vision. She leans to the side, allows the blood to touch her cheek. It is the closest thing to touching her daughter, I guess. Nancy follows the flow of blood, and that is when she sees the silhouette of Kristopher.

Her eyes track the rope over the beam. It wraps around her belly.

"Kristopher?"

She stands, cheek shining with blood. She inches forward and the body lowers in concert. Understanding the connection, she takes two purposeful strides.

Kristopher crumbles as if his bones are made of taffy. (Making myself hungry again!) Nancy gasps at the sight. She does not see the thin rope running at ankle height between two pillars.

Here we go, rounding the corner and scaling a stack of books at the same time. It can get messy here. Every error is redeemable, mind you, but there is a certain beauty in a plan coming to fruition exactly as envisioned. My stomach is full of roiling snakes. Everything has been perfect.

Come on Nancy. Be perfect for me.

Her right ankle touches the thin rope, and her mind blocks the sensation from registering. She falls in slow motion, duct tape mittens raised to protect her face. The obelisk on the coffee table disappears as the glass shatters. It is an explosion of sound and then nothing, a few shards of glass tinkling.

Nancy is still. No expression of pain or gasps for breath.

"Nancy?"

Glass crunching. She shakes like a newborn calf finding its legs.

"Nancy?"

She cannot lift her body and instead turns her head. The obelisk juts from her cheek, eye above it filled with blood the color of strawberry jelly.

It should be enough.

Her face looks like a Halloween mask tossed in a blender set to pulse. The glass in her right eye has Doug's cum on it. She opens her mouth to speak and blows blood bubbles at me.

Here we are again, the last domino.

What is it, Nancy?

What do you want your last words in this life to be?

"Why?" she gurgles.

Oh Nancy.

IF HE IS NOTHING ELSE, DOUG IS CONSISTENT. HE NEVER spends more than eight minutes jacking off in the office parking lot. He always arrives within five minutes of five o'clock.

5:01 PM, Doug parks his sedan, loosens his tie. He does not see me parked across the street. They never do.

He walks through the front door and at that moment I can guess his movement through the house. He calls for Nancy and the kids. With no response he tries Nancy's cell and hears it ringing in the master bedroom. He dials the kids' phones and finds one on the dining room table and the other in a bedroom.

Nothing is out of place. Nancy's tooth is safely tucked away in my fannypack. With no additional real estate to explore, Doug migrates to the basement (man cave) door. Maybe the wife and kids went for a walk. It's never happened before, but Nancy's been on a health kick lately. (For the Amazon guy, not you, Doug)

He will try to save them. He will lift Kaylee off the blade, cut the seven miles of duct tape from her arms and legs. Her blood was cool when I left, but Doug won't notice. He'll pull Nancy out of her coffee table prison, swallowing uncomfortably at the cloudy glass speckling her face. He'll cut the rope from Kristopher's neck, probably slicing the skin in the process.

He'll run his fingers through his hair. He'll pace the room, walking bloody shoeprints halfway up the stairs before returning to the bodies, checking for pulses again. He'll touch *everything.*

He will not call for help.

Not if he is like the others.

It's 5:23, Doug, what are you waiting for? Writing a note, probably. At some point he will recognize his predicament. Doug is the office weirdo. He knows this. He doesn't know there are security cameras in the parking lot. Everyone knows what Doug does in the morning. They don't have a clean picture of it, just footage of the sedan with fogged up windows rocking back and forth for no more than eight minutes.

Even without that knowledge, it doesn't look good. The office weirdo with his DNA all over the scene. What are you doing Doug? Running a magnet over your covert porn tapes?

I reach inside my fannypack but find only crumbs.

5:31 I hear the gunshot.

5:32 a second gunshot.

Good old reliable Doug. Either the first shot was a test, as he likely had never fired the gun before, or the bullet failed to end his life.

I hope for the latter.

WHY?

That is the only question that matters, isn't it?

It is the question they ask even with the echoes of their dying children in their ears.

If I told you it was my favorite thing to do in the whole, wide world would it be enough?

No.

You want to know why I picked you. What makes you special?

Well, maybe you'll have an opportunity to ask me yourself.

THE LAST CHANCE DINER

The desert night stretched before them like a gray blanket. Occasionally, the swath cast by the headlights caught a glimpse of roadside detritus. Tumbleweeds waiting for new wind, carrion turning to dust. There were mountains somewhere in the distance, far beyond the reach of the lights, and very little else. It might have been desert. It might have been Mars.

Beneath the tires the road thrummed, a steady drone interrupted by the occasional jolt from cracks in the asphalt. The sky glittered above, split into halves by the champagne-colored band of the Milky Way. There was no moon, only stars, and too many of them to count before sunrise.

"I'm getting hungry," Zac said, his voice barely audible over the drone.

"What's that?" Josh risked a glance at Zac for a change in scenery.

He'd been drifting for miles, muscle memory and a dim awareness of reality keeping the Tahoe in its lane. There were no opposing headlights to track and no radio to distract, just a crackling sound coming through the speakers, like bacon on a griddle. It would have been so easy to just fall asleep. If Zac hadn't spoken he might have.

"Do we have any road-food left?" Zac said, unbuckling his seatbelt to inspect the backseat.

"No clue," Josh said. His road-weary eyes drifted to the dashboard clock. It was just past midnight. Josh did not remember if he'd adjusted it when crossing time zones. Regardless, if there was nothing left in the Tahoe to eat, they were probably out of luck.

"Find anything?" Josh asked as Zac settled back into his seat.

"Just a bag of garbage," Zac said, wiping his hand on his jeans.

"Can you last until breakfast?"

"I guess. Maybe I'm more bored than hungry. Can't get a signal out here. Nothing to listen to."

Josh pushed his glasses up the bridge of his nose to settle in the crease there. He couldn't remember the last meal he'd eaten. He couldn't remember what state they were in.

He remembered driving.

Only driving.

Behind him was Tennessee. Behind him was a family who spat his own words back to him as if the syllables were poison. Peppered in the conversation were references to books of the Bible and words of hate.

His words might as well have been a different language. There was no understanding.

His father paced, hands clasped as if he did not trust himself to free them. Josh remembered his father nodding his head and leaving the room without making eye contact. His mother cried and begged them to stay.

Then the drive. Kansas felt like forever. A rainbow somewhere in Colorado. They took it as a sign and chased the setting sun.

They must have eaten somewhere along the way. He just couldn't remember it.

"Do you smell that?" Zac asked.

"What?"

"Something cooking," he said, sitting up in his seat, nose near the air vent. "Look!"

How had either of them missed it? There was nothing else in front of them, just the desert and a brilliant spot of light illuminating a diner. A sign glowed over the entrance: *Last Chance Diner*

"Was there a sign for it before?" Zac asked.

"I didn't see one."

Josh shifted his foot from the gas to the brake and flipped the turn signal on. The restaurant could have been built in the nineteen fifties. It had that forced retro-futuristic appearance, all rounded angles, and chrome. The parking lot was about half-filled. Josh found a spot large enough to accommodate their vehicle and parked.

"We going in?" Josh asked.

Zac shrugged, already climbing out of the SUV, "Maybe just get dessert?"

Josh shook his head with a smile and followed behind, shrugging a little deeper into his hoodie to keep the dessert chill at bay.

A bell chimed to announce their arrival. The lights in the restaurant were bright, brighter than they needed to be. Josh shielded his eyes as they adjusted but sensed the radiance penetrating his eyelids. A dozen heads turned toward the new arrivals, folks sitting alone and a family of four. The décor inside the restaurant was predictably kitschy: posters of Elvis and Marilyn Monroe on the walls; the tiles were black and white. Deep teals dominated everything else.

They passed a sign requesting they seat themselves and obeyed its directive, sliding into the nearest unoccupied booth. There was music playing, but the signal faded in and out, alternating between an oldies station that matched the vibe of the restaurant, and a religious program featuring a raspy-voiced preacher. The only clear word he spoke, through bursts of static, was *sin*.

A waitress approached, smiling, red lipstick peeling from her lips. The clusters of tight lines above her mouth indicated she was a smoker or had been. Her hair was a box job, a red that might have matched her lipstick the first few weeks after application. It was more of an auburn then, the roots stark white.

"What can I get you boys to drink?"

Zac looked up from his menu and placed a hand to his heart. He inspected her face, squinting over the frame of his glasses.

"I'll have a water with lemon," Josh said, not taking his eyes off the menu.

The silence persisted, the waitress holding a yellow pencil above her notepad.

"And you, sugar?"

Zac cleared his throat. "I'm sorry. You just remind me of someone. My grandma. She's been gone for a few years now. Spitting image though, just wasn't expecting it."

"Oh, I look like lots of people's grandmas I imagine," she said, squeezing his shoulder with a wink.

Zac shook his head as if to clear it, "Just a water for now. No lemon, thank you."

She didn't bother writing it down but nodded her head with a smile.

"Be right back."

Josh studied the laminated menu but looked up when Zac tapped his hand.

"She looks just like her. *Just.* I mean. She looks like her twin."

Josh considered how much interest he should show, attempting to select the right combination of words that would satisfy Zac without prompting further conversation on the matter.

He settled on, "That's weird."

"Super weird! I might try to sneak a picture of her before we leave."

Josh nodded, waiting to see if that was the end of the discussion.

"Why are you squinting like that?"

"Am I?" Josh removed his glasses and rubbed his eyes with a knuckle. "It's the light in here. It's so bright. Feels like I'm staring at the sun."

"Think so?"

Josh blinked a few times, "Probably just tired. We should switch after we're done here. I'll nap a bit."

For a minute, neither spoke. Despite the myriad options, and his apparent honest assessment of them, Josh decided on his usual order of a cheeseburger and fries. Zac settled on pie but wanted the waitress' opinion about which was best.

She returned with the water as Josh stacked their menus. Zac fumbled with his phone to sneak a picture but realized it would be too obvious to try in that moment. Perhaps if he applied his charm, he could simply request one.

"You boys ready?"

"I'll have the cheeseburger and fries," Josh said.

"All the way?"

"Unless that includes boiled cabbage for some reason," Josh handed her the menus.

She winked, "Not today it doesn't."

"I'm thinking I want pie," Zac said when she looked to him. "If you had to pick, which would you choose?"

The waitress nibbled on the pencil's eraser before answering, "I'm partial to pecan pie, myself. But apple's our biggest seller. They serve it with a slice of cheddar on the side, like they do up north."

"Oh, I've never had it like that. I'll do apple."

She took his menu and moved to pivot away, but stopped herself, turning instead to place a hand on Zac's arm.

"It's good to see you," she said, and turned to Josh. "You too, young man."

When she was out of earshot Zac whispered, "That was weird! I mean, it was sweet but weird."

Josh shrugged. "Maybe hoping for a good tip. Can't exactly flirt with us..."

Most of the customers were elderly and lost within their own worlds, stirring soup long after it stopped steaming. The family at the opposite end of the restaurant was quiet despite the presence of two sub-ten-year-old kids. Of the terms he would use to describe the other diners, wealthy was not among them. Tips were probably thin way out in the desert. Being extra friendly might the only way the poor woman survived.

"Do you hear that?" Josh asked, taking his glasses off again and placing a hand over his eyes to block the overhead light.

Zac cocked his head.

"The radio? It's between two stations I think."

Josh shook his head.

"Something else. Like a drone. I can hear the music and the preacher, but there's another sound beneath that."

After half a minute of listening Zac shook his head.

Josh looked around. No one else appeared disturbed by the noise, either.

"Does this place feel off to you?" Josh asked.

As Zac faced the entrance to the restaurant, he was only able to see a few of the customers. He stretched, glancing behind as he did. None of the customers huddled over cell phones, not that they could get a signal out here. There were none of the expected sounds from the kitchen, clanking of spatulas, sizzling of meat.

When he looked back to Josh he shrugged again, "That's just diners, isn't it?"

"What about that?" Josh nodded toward the bar area. There was a long painting above it, a serene, stylized rendition of the interior of the restaurant.

Zac looked, "What about it?"

It did not show a bustling establishment with svelte waitresses balancing loaded trays. No attractive couples on double dates laughing over a shared milkshake. Instead, there were unoccupied chairs and empty booths. Just a family, a few elderly people seated alone, and...

"Josh, look at the booth nearest the exit," Zac said.

He gripped Josh's forearm.

There were two men in the booth seated across from each other. One wore a black hoodie and the other a checkered, short-sleeved shirt.

"Is that..." Josh began.

"It looks like it," Zac said.

Josh surveyed the restaurant, comparing it to the scene captured in the painting. An old man wearing a fishing hat two booths blew the steam from a bowl of chili. A middle-aged woman with a cup of coffee. The family of four near the bathrooms. They all matched the painting.

"What is that smell? I don't think it's food," Zac said.

It was the same smell as in the Tahoe.

Josh flexed his jaw, trying to pop his ears, "You sure you don't hear it?"

Zac shook his head. He joined Josh on the opposite side of the booth to get a better view of the restaurant and its occupants.

The waitress crossed the tile floor, a plate of bacon and eggs in her hand, a bowl of grits balanced on her forearm. She placed the items in front of an elderly black man wearing an oil-stained mechanic's work shirt. He jolted at her appearance, but softened as she engaged in conversation, placing a hand on his shoulder. When she left, he watched her go with a smile aimed somewhere over her head, beyond the walls of the restaurant likely.

"Zac, look at the painting," Josh said, still massaging his temples. The drone in his head competed in volume with the intermittent music. The lights were still far too bright.

Though it had been empty save for a napkin dispenser and a cup of coffee a minute ago, the man in the painting now gazed at a plate of eggs and bacon on his table, a bowl of grits sitting off to the side.

And the man in the checkered shirt now sat next to the man in the hoodie.

"It can't be …" he said, staring in disbelief. "What does this mean?"

Josh had no answers. He was no longer hungry. He wanted to be on the road. He wanted to be driving again, putting distance between himself and everything else.

"I don't know," he said. "I can't really think right now. I'm tired. My eyes hurt. That noise is so loud I can barely hear you."

Zac laced his fingers within Josh's, afraid his hand would begin shaking otherwise.

The waitress returned.

She held an old-fashioned rotary phone, red, like her lipstick. "Josh?"

"Yes?" he answered, squinting as if the light behind her was the sun.

"Phone for you, dear."

There were no cords leading to it. It was just the phone.

"Excuse me?"

"Phone for you," she said, smiling and nodding as she held it out to him.

Josh took the phone and placed it to his ear.

"H—hello?"

There was a sigh from the other end, "I wish I could tell you I'm sorry, son."

The connection fizzled and popped, growing fuzzy before fading back in. Josh struggled to hear over the incessant droning.

"Dad?"

The voice was ragged, a throaty whisper, like his dad had been crying. Something Josh had never seen him do. It sounded like his dad was saying something else, but it was buried in the static.

"I love you. Always. I always loved you. I-I just wasn't raised right I guess," he said.

"Dad, it's okay. What's going on? How did you reach me here?" Josh felt like he was shouting to be heard. Zac looked away from him for a moment, drawing Josh's eye up to the painting.

The man in the painting, the one in the black hoodie, held a red phone to his ear.

Another rush of crackling static.

"I'm sorry, son. I'm just so damn sorry."

"Dad? Dad!"

With a loud pop, the crackling ended, and the line went dead. The waitress appeared, hands extended to retrieve the phone.

"What was that? How did your dad know we were here? What did he want?"

Josh raked his fingers through his hair.

"I don't know. He just, just said he was sorry. He was sorry and he loved me."

They were silent for a while before Zac spoke again.

"What is this place?"

Josh sat up straight and cleared his throat. The room was so bright he had to keep his eyes shut.

"What's the last thing you remember?"

"Before this? Colorado, I think. There was the rainbow in the spray of the waterfall. I think I remember the sign for Utah. Probably dozed after that …"

It was so bright, and the drone was so loud. Loud as the horn of an eighteen-wheeler.

"That's about the last thing I remember, too. Then I started to get sleepy. Turned the radio on. Couldn't find a station. Just some oldies and a religious show," Josh said, turning to face Zac.

"What are you saying?"

The waitress returned and slid Josh's plate across the table. She placed the pie in front of Zac and retreated a step.

"Get you boys anything else?"

They were no longer hungry. It didn't really smell like food. It smelled like burning rubber and motor oil.

"Where are we?" Josh asked her, nudging his plate away.

The waitress offered the front of her notepad, which presumably bore the restaurant's name. Josh couldn't see it clearly, though. He only saw the light.

"Where are we, really?" Zac asked.

"Sugar, you're just passin' through."

She left with a wink, disappearing through the swinging door to the kitchen.

"Look," Zac said elbowing Josh.

"I can't. What is it?"

"The painting. There are people missing." He twisted beside Josh before settling again. "They're not in the restaurant either."

"They're gone?"

"The man with the hat. The family. They're all gone."

With a final flare, the bright light faded. The roar in his ears subsided. Josh blinked and glanced around the room as it came back into focus.

"Are we…"

"I think so," Zac said.

Their hands met again, holding fast.

Josh nibbled on a french fry. The burger, despite being the *Best West of the Mississippi!*, was not so appealing.

"I'm sorry," he said as tears welled.

"You don't have to be," Zac said.

He paired the cheddar cheese with the apple pie in a single bite.

"Why not?"

Zac chewed, his delight in the competing flavors evident on his face.

"Because we're still together. Isn't that what this move was about, anyway?"

The waitress returned and Zac was quite certain if he called her by his grandmother's name, she would respond to it.

"How was everything?" she asked, hands on her hips.

"Perfect. Just what I needed," Zac said.

Josh sucked in a breath. "Ma'am, where do we go now?"

She smiled at him and reached across the table to brush a hand over the fine hairs of his cheek.

"Sugar, you just go home."

No Gods Only Chaos – The title is pulled from a line our "old god" speaks in the story "Offerings to an Old God." To me, it is the perfect representation of my thoughts regarding the horror genre. *Gods* can represent many things, but foremost is *order*. Order as in structure, something one can predict or rely on like the position of the stars in the sky or the changing of the seasons. *Chaos*, then, is what interrupts the order. These four words, combined, are extremely unsettling to me. It means there is no order, no structure. The peace you feel at any given moment only exists because the chaos has not found you.

Not yet.

The cover art is inspired by my own interpretation of the concept of *as above, so below*. Some take a religious perspective of this phrase, others more metaphysical and even astrological. To me, this represents balance and my belief that our spiritual evolution is not toward perfection but completion.

STORY NOTES

CEMETERY JOE – THIS IS A VERY IMPORTANT STORY FOR ME, as it was my first pro sale. Joe (unrelated) from Cemetery Gates posted on Twitter about this entry, as I originally submitted it under the more provocative title "Corpse Fucker Joe." That post caught the eye of Sadie Hartmann, who soon saw my name come through her slush pile with the story "The Bystander," which was accepted for publication in the Human Monsters anthology. It also sparked a dialogue leading to the publication of my novella, *Stargazers*. The story itself came together fairly organically. I appreciate themed story calls as they narrow my focus when writing. The idea of having to retrieve an object from the town creep's hovel has been done before, so I wanted to take it in a different direction after that initial set-up. I tend to pull back in stories, coming to the precipice of uncomfortable situations only to ease off the gas at the last minute. For Cemetery Joe, I pressed the pedal to the floor.

HESITATION CUTS – SOME PHRASES STAY WITH YOU. I'VE HAD the term *hesitation cuts* rolling around in my head for years, but never had a story that fit until this one. This is among the most disturbing things I've written. I built the story around the idea of a man losing control of his faculties and suspecting his wife is an imposter. I shifted my writing style to accommodate his perception, repeating certain phrases and disrupting his interpretation of the passage of time. *Spoiler – As the story is from the perspective of a man who is drifting from reality, the ending is intentionally confused. Anna was aware of his mental degradation. The needlepoint project she was working on was a final anniversary gift before releasing our main character to the care he required.

THE BYSTANDER – ANOTHER EXAMPLE OF WRITING WITHOUT limits. I had the idea for my human monster, Avery, and began writing the story from the moment he picks up Gary 2. Adding Avery's history, and weaving it into the narrative of the story, changed the tone. I hoped readers would be shocked at what they found funny in what is a quite brutal scenario. For me, the humor comes through in the small details, the fixation on food and names as examples. It demonstrates our main character is entirely focused on the wrong things.

FROM THE RED DIRT – I HAVE AN AFFINITY FOR AMERICA'S Dust Bowl era. Using it as a setting almost feels like cheating in a way, because the bleak setting, the dire circumstances are established at the onset. This was a submission to a zombie anthology, and of course I wanted to take mine in a different direction. A classic zombie is a being, formerly living, returned from the dead. Typically, this is for a nefarious purpose, regardless of the zombie's awareness of the havoc it wreaks. For this story, the return from the dead was the result of grandfather's love for his family. I enjoyed playing with the language, truncating words and simplifying the speech to match that of a poorly educated boy of the time and region. Like many of my stories, I set out to write something brutal or horrifying and found myself gravitating toward the heart at the center of the tale.

UNDER NO CIRCUMSTANCES – THIS WAS THE B-SIDE TO Cemetery Joe. I was so certain I'd missed the mark with Cemetery Joe, including its original title, I quickly wrote another graveyard story I thought was a bit tempered. I find the idea of mankind's prehistory very seductive. It's this blank space hundreds of thousands of years long. What were they like? What did they believe in? Could they have believed in something real that no longer exists, or exists on the periphery? These questions and a cemetery setting got me started.

URBEX – I WROTE THIS FOR A BUG-RELATED ANTHOLOGY, and it was not accepted. I liked it enough to include it in this collection as its perspective on introspection is unique compared to the other stories. I often include details in a story without understanding why. These become threads I later pull on and find a more substantial meaning. I included the main character's history with illness without understanding where it would lead. As the story progressed, I realized the abandoned facility was representative of the character's body, her eventual acceptance of her mortality. Originally, this was intended to be body horror. I planned to really go for it with the cockroaches. The closer I came to those moments in the story, however, the less needed they were.

OFFERINGS TO AN OLD GOD – THE THEME OF THIS STORY was *monster lairs*. Upon reading the editor's requirements/wishes, I understood a modern setting would not work for the rough idea I had. I also did not want to dedicate half of a short story to world building. There is a fair amount of exposition as is. For the monster, I thought of something in the vein of Shelob from The Lord of the Rings. But Shelob already exists, and I don't find a giant spider particularly frightening. I went more cosmic with the monster's origins as the idea of the infinite terrifies me. In retrospect, the story owes a debt to Shirley Jackson's The Lottery, in the sense it is a community sacrificing its children without a true understanding of why. The god in the story simply took what was offered.

THE FINAL GIFT – WRITTEN FOR A CONTEST IN WHICH YOU are given a genre, setting, and an object that must be included in the story. I forget what the object was, but I know for certain it was not the cuckoo clock. That was included because my daughter was very much into cuckoo clocks at the time. Luckily, she moved on to other interests before we were forced to buy one.

THE LAST OF OUR KIND – I HAD HIGH HOPES FOR THIS story. I wrote it months in advance of its submission due date, sent it to writer friends second and third opinions. The project was delayed several times and then fell apart. It's a hefty story and there weren't any viable options for it in the aftermath of the project's dissolution. Name-dropping her again, but it was Sadie Hartmann's comments about a lack of *girls on bikes* stories that propelled my imagination. I had a half-formed idea about desert vampires, something novella-length, that never solidified into a cohesive story. But I liked the setting. Like 30 Days of Night, changing the setting makes a huge difference in the story you tell. I feel like there is a novella's worth of story to tell. Maybe I'll come back to this someday.

ONLY EVER NIGHT – SOMETIMES IT'S JUST A SINGLE IMAGE. I've written stories based on a line from a song or a phrase in a book. I built this story around the image of the disappearing egg. This is also the oldest story in the collection, written for a non-paying anthology, which also offered no critical oversight. Therefore, it underwent a heavy edit for this collection. It's the same story as was included in the anthology, just reworked. I did not offer many explanations. In a short story there often is not room to do so. I would say The Langoliers was somewhere in the back of my mind while writing this.

THE RETURN OF THE CHAMPION – ALSO AN OLDER STORY. I do not recall the anthology it was intended for. Like Only Ever Night, this underwent a substantial edit prior to including it in this collection. Rereading after not having thought about it for a couple years, I saw what I was going for and also where I fell short in execution. In the back of my mind, I was probably processing some emotions from extended separations from my wife and children due to my military service. The main character has my wife's name, after all.

FAMILY ANNIHILATOR − THERE IS A CONNECTIVE THREAD between The Bystander and Family Annihilator. I wrote The Bystander first and enjoyed being in the headspace of someone incapable of empathy. Don't read too much into that. It's fun to write. Please do not add me to any surveillance lists. When this anthology opportunity came around, I felt there was still some juice left to squeeze in an emotionless killer. For this main character, I did not pull back the curtains on his motivation. It was not as important to me as the acts of violence he commits. However, the care he takes in not being the person holding the knife, or pulling the trigger, suggests there is something there. He is cold blooded, but not a monolith. Similar to The Bystander, I had fun injecting humor into what is a very grim scenario.

THE LAST CHANCE DINER − AKA THE PALLET CLEANSER. I wrote this with two of my best friends in mind.

ABOUT THE AUTHOR

L.P. HERNANDEZ IS THE AUTHOR OF TWO PREVIOUS SHORT story collections, *Dreadful: Tales of the Dead and Dying*, and *The Rat King*. His novella, *Stargazers*, kicked off the *My Dark Library* line of novellas published by Cemetery Gates Media. He is also a regular contributor to The NoSleep Podcast. When not writing, he serves as a medical administrator in the United States Air Force. He is married to the love of his life, Miranda, and his two favorite kids are the ones he helped create, Maggie and Yoss. He is a dog person, loves heavy metal and a crisp high five.